A Dog Called Valentine

A Dog Called Valentine

Roxanne Snopek

A Dog Called Valentine

Tule Publishing First Printing, January 2019

The Tule Publishing, Inc.

First Publication by Tule Publishing 2019

ISBN: 978-1-949707-71-7

CHAPTER ONE

"CONGRATULATIONS! YOU'VE BEEN approved," said the text message. "Here's your match. Please contact us at your earliest convenience for details. Have a great day!"

Lily Garner stared at her cell phone for a moment, and then leaped up from her chair and gave a whoop, sending a sheaf of term project reports cascading to the floor.

The woman in the cubicle next to her shrieked, then sagged back in relief. "Lily, you're going to give me a heart attack one of these days. This better be good."

"It is," Lily told her. She came around the side of the narrow divider, holding the small screen out for her friend to see. "They found me a match! I knew this was the right thing to do. Just look at him, Harp. He's perfect. Oh, I can't wait to meet him."

Harpreet Kaur shifted her glossy black hair over one shoulder, peered at the screen and made a face. "You're giving up, is that it? My cousin has a friend—"

"Harp, I love you like a sister, but the last dinner date you set me up with, some friend of a cousin's roommate's high-school buddy or whatever, talked for forty-five minutes straight without asking me a single question. About accounting. Actually, it was longer than that, but I didn't start timing him right away. He sent his steak back twice, and then didn't leave a tip. He was the worst date, ever. And I've dated a lot of losers."

Harpreet waved a hand. "This one's different."

Lily perched a hip on her friend and coinstructor's desk. "You always say that. Everyone says that. I'm tired of it. No more eharmony, no more Match.com, no more setups by well-meaning friends and relatives."

Harpreet tipped her head at the wedding photo pinned to her wall. "Setups can work."

Lily swallowed, turning her gaze to the happy couple. She'd been the maid of honor during the week of events culminating in Harp and Manny's multicultural celebration. "I know. But your parents introduced you to someone awesome." She shuddered. "My mother…"

Harpreet put up a hand. "This is a safe space. She Who Must Not Be Named is not welcome here."

A face peered over the divider, blue eyes wide with curiosity. Danika Shubert, the third part of their art and design program triumvirate. "What am I missing? Are we talking about Lily's love life? Ooh, catch me up."

Harpreet leaned back in her seat. "Lily's given up on love."

"I have not!"

"I was afraid that would happen." Danika crossed yoga-toned arms above the swell of her baby bump and pursed her lips. "It's time for an intervention."

"No intervention!"

But it was as if they didn't even hear her.

"Perhaps a party? Wait. I know." Harpreet's mouth held the o sound, as excitement took hold. "We need to celebrate our new venture! We'll do it at our house, invite everyone we know—"

"No party." Lily stepped between them, holding her palms up like a traffic cop. "No intervention. No need for mass hysteria or running in the streets and eating brains. Definitely not about us starting our own firm. My mother thinks teaching design is bad enough—"

"No mother talk," Harpreet insisted.

Danika nodded. "She makes you crazy and this is a crazy-free zone. Now, back to you giving up on love?"

Lily exhaled loudly. "I'm taking a break from dating, that's all. Geez. Just because you two are both paired up like pigeons doesn't mean I have to quickly dive for the nearest single guy, like he's a chair and the music's about to stop. It'll happen when it happens and probably when I least expect it. Or, it won't. I'm fine, either way."

She stopped for breath and looked down, suddenly unable to meet her friends' eyes.

Danika put a hand on her arm. "Honey," she said softly, her voice full of kindness, "you're more than fine. You're beautiful and interesting and accomplished and kind and so talented."

"Stop." Lily adjusted her shoulders and made herself smile. "It's not like I have a broken heart. It's time for a change, that's all. Something completely different. I was just telling Harp about it. Look."

She pulled up the photo again and held her phone out.

"You're done with dating," Danika said, "but that appeals to you?"

"That's what I said," crowed Harpreet. "Talk about homely."

"Talk about home*less*." Danika shook her head. "Really, Lily? This seems rather impulsive."

"He's had all his shots and he's neutered, which would normally be a deal breaker but in this case is exactly right."

"Oh, honey," Danika said.

"He's a dog," Harpreet said.

"Yes, he is," Lily said, "and don't worry, I'm not keeping him. He's just staying with me until he finds his forever home. A month or two, tops."

"You'll get fleas," Harpreet said.

"Bad idea," Danika said.

"I don't care," Lily said.

Then she hugged each of her friends and turned back to her phone to look again at the photo of her soon-to-be foster dog.

SOME DAYS YOU'RE the hammer and some days you're the nail.

And some days, thought Shane Bowman, shaking his

hand, you're an idiot who doesn't know when to lay down the tools and watch TV.

The fresh throb in his thumb joined the chorus from his shoulder, currently hitting high notes thanks to the hour of pain and torture he'd had that morning.

His physical therapist had no sense of humor.

"You okay in there, Shane, honey?"

His grandmother, who owned the one-hundred-year-old heritage home he was working on, had stopped in to check on the progress, thoughtfully bringing a vat of soup that would feed him for a week.

"Nothing TSN and a cold beer can't fix," he called back.

Gram laughed. "Good try. Supper's ready. Come eat. It's starting soon."

It, meaning *The Bachelorette.* Recorded, so they could share at their leisure, since he had no other plans.

Nothing wrong with Gram's sense of humor.

"I'd rather drop a hatchet on my foot, Gram," he replied.

She poked her head around the corner. Yoga and aerobics at the seniors' complex where she now lived kept her fit and she proudly owned her gray hair and wrinkles, saying she'd earned every single one of them.

"Didn't you just do that?"

"That was my thumb. And a hammer."

She snorted. "Matter of time. Now, go wash up. Soup and bread. It's all set up."

Gram never missed an episode, even if it meant watching it on her old set, in her old kitchen, surrounded by tarps, tools, sawhorses and dust.

He stood up, wincing as his arm protested the change of position. He was grateful she trusted him with this restoration, but reality TV was a high price.

He went to the powder room and leaned on the sink, looking into the cracked, pitted mirror. Dark circles under his eyes betrayed broken sleep, but the gaunt cheeks were filled out and the gray sheen of pain was mostly replaced by the flush and sweat of honest work. Gram's meals, physical labor and mandated exercise were all rebuilding him, but it was slow work.

He splashed water on his face, not worried about the drops that landed on the ancient wallpaper. Removing it was next on his list and wasn't that going to be a treat? The tiny washroom, nestled beneath the peaked cottage roof, was a collection of angles that would make Picasso proud. Who put wallpaper in a bathroom, let alone one that required so much geometry?

Idiosyncrasies like this were what made this house so special. And would, when he was finally done, attract the right buyer, someone who would love it the way generations of Bowmans had loved it.

He looked out the hexagonal stained-glass window and onto the yard, noticing that the rungs he and Ben had nailed onto the trunk of the old oak were still there. The paths they'd worn into the grassy slope heading down to the river, however, had long since grown over, replaced by the footprints of other children.

They hadn't appreciated the size of the yard then, of course. It was just Gram and Gramp's house, a vast playground inside as well as out. Even at Christmas, they'd played hide-and-seek outdoors among the shrubs, glorying in the balmy weather that was so different from that of their snowy Prince George home.

Ben was as happy as he was that Gram's house wouldn't be torn down to make way for some monstrous contemporary mansion. There was history in those walls, good history.

If not for him, Gram would have already sold the place, as is. Instead, she took it off the market, gave him somewhere to live and a reason to get up in the mornings. He only hoped her trust wasn't misplaced.

He cranked the faucet handle, reminding himself to buy new washers to fix the drip. Structural repairs and updates to the antiquated plumbing and wiring had all been completed, but some things, like the gold-toned fixtures and glass doorknobs, simply couldn't be replaced without altering the character of the home.

Within the next two months, three tops, he would be done.

"Shane!" she called again. "Soup's getting cold."

"Coming."

He ran a hand through his hair and stared at himself again, fighting back the familiar question. When he was done here, what would he do with the rest of his life?

The question had plagued him for seventeen months, two weeks, six days and, he glanced at his watch, forty minutes, give or take.

He thought he'd been the hammer that day, a tool in the long, strong arm of the law, ready to come down on crime, to bring a bad, bad man to justice.

Instead, he'd been the nail, hit hard, stopped dead.

And now he was stuck.

He rubbed his right shoulder, where the bullet had entered, shattering bone, ripping muscle and tendon, leaving him unable to hold a gun steady, unsafe to fire it.

A stupid, stinking, career-ending shoulder injury.

The docs told him he'd been lucky. A few inches lower and toward his heart and he'd have bled out.

"Enough," he muttered. He pushed away the memories and walked through the narrow hallway to the kitchen.

"There you are," Gram said. She patted the chair beside her. An ancient metal folding TV tray sat in front of it, holding a bowl of thick, meaty soup and a large slab of butter-drenched bread, fresh from the oven.

Gram had her electronic tablet open and was tapping the keyboard, her red-framed glasses balanced on the tip of her nose. "What year did you complete your training, dear?"

There was only one reason she'd be asking for such details.

"Gram. We've been over this." He dug into his bowl. Delicious.

She lifted her head and peered through the lenses, her eyes huge with magnification and innocence. "I'm just asking. My memory isn't what it used to be." Her voice was full of indignation.

He dipped a chunk of bread into the rich broth. "No getting your friends to do your dirty work, either."

Her cronies were just as bad as she was, when it came to his single status.

Silence. He'd found her loophole.

What was worse than your grandmother and seven of her gal pals ogling half-naked young men on a beach?

Having them nominate you for a spot on the show.

But he watched the program with her while he ate and even found himself laughing at the antics of some of the contestants.

"You know," Gram said during a commercial break, "if you fixed yourself up, instead of spending every waking minute on this house, we could sell you, too. In a flash." She snapped her fingers.

"Some people call that prostitution."

She ignored him. "It's not right, a handsome young man, alone and lonely. You need someone to enjoy your life with. Someone who can make you smile again."

She got up and stirred the big pot on the stove, which stood in the middle of the room, back-to-back with the refrigerator. The huge apron-front farmhouse sink remained functional, also, in its position beneath the window overlooking the backyard. But the rest of the room was gutted.

Kind of like him.

"I smile." He gave her a toothy grin.

"That's not a smile. It's a cry for help. Finish your

borscht and let me at least send in your photo."

"Forget it, Gram. You and Gramps found each other the old-fashioned way. You had sixty years together, raised five kids, and never had a harsh word between you."

"So naive." She patted his cheek and sighed. "Your grandfather and I had plenty of harsh words. I locked him out of the house once. Threw all his clothes onto the lawn."

"What? Why?" Shane couldn't even imagine it.

She laughed. "I don't remember. But we always made up. Your father would tell you. Talking it over got us through some hard times." She picked up her empty bowl. "You should at least get another dog."

Shane froze. "Gram."

"I know, I know. There will never be another Titan. But you could get a different kind of dog, one that doesn't remind you of him so much, maybe."

"Gram." He ground his teeth together, then exhaled slowly. "I don't want to talk about it."

"Okay, fine." She huffed. "I hear Tanya is engaged."

Oh, God. She was on a roll tonight, if she was invoking the name of his former fiancée.

"Good for her. I hope she's very happy." His enthusiasm sounded hollow, but he meant it. Tanya deserved a man who loved her with his whole heart.

The show resumed then, and for once, Shane was grateful.

It took a lot to make people hate a man who'd nearly died while protecting and serving, but breaking Tanya's heart had done it. If Gram thought this news might encourage him to go home when the renovation was finished, she was wrong.

Titan was dead.

Shane was no longer a cop.

He wasn't getting married.

Prince George wasn't home anymore.

Chapter Two

LILY LOOKED AT the pink-and-black collar and matching leash she'd picked out at the pet store. She knew the shelter would provide what she needed for the dog she'd be looking after, but she couldn't resist. It coordinated so well with her favorite jogging outfit, a waterproof hooded jacket and matching pants in black and pink. If she was going to be outside walking a dog during the darkest, wettest time of the year, she might as well look good doing it.

She volunteered at the shelter regularly, but this was her first time taking her work home with her, so to speak, and she was both excited and nervous. Though she loved animals, she hadn't had one herself before. But her students were completing their projects now and the new cohort didn't begin until March, so she had a lovely break to catch her breath and recalibrate her life.

She looked again at the photo of the dog. It wasn't very clear. Ariel, the shelter manager, had told her he'd be ready to go home with her at the end of her volunteer shift this morning.

When her cell phone rang, she grabbed it, then winced, seeing the caller ID.

"Good morning, Mother."

"Oh, Lily."

Three small syllables. The soundtrack of her life.

She steeled herself not to react. "I'm heading to the shelter soon. Was there something you needed?"

As chief purse-string-holder of one of Vancouver's largest private charitable foundations, Marisa Kovac Garner Rollins spent her days deciding where to donate her money and encouraging others to follow suit. Her nod could deem a cause worthy, turn a hopeful up-and-comer into a star, create a trend, or smother a fad. Her social capital had launched many a career.

Not Lily's, of course. Interior design was too close to construction work, in Marisa's opinion. Not to mention, a reminder of husband number one.

"Yes!" Marisa's voice shook. "Sissy Hartwick just told me that her son told her that you told him you wouldn't be having dinner with him again."

Marisa's deepest desire was for Lily to take her rightful place in society—with the right man at her side.

Unfortunately, Lily and her mother didn't agree on what constituted an ideal man any more than they did about what constituted an ideal career.

"Chad was very nice, Mom. But we have nothing in common."

"Did you even try to get to know him?"

Lily pressed two fingers against the space between her eyebrows. "If it's not there, it's not there."

Marisa sounded near tears. "But this is important to me. Chad is coming to the benefit and he will not want to go alone. You represent the Kovac Foundation. How many times do I have to tell you?"

Guilt, her old friend, assailed Lily. Her mother's life hadn't been easy. The Kovac Foundation meant everything to her. Frank Garner, Lily's father, had been killed in a construction accident when she was twelve and Sara fourteen, leaving Marisa widowed, if not entirely bereaved. The marriage had been rocky, with Marisa aiming far higher than Frank's blue-collar lifestyle. Life insurance plus a generous settlement from the company responsible for the faulty equipment had left Marisa and her daughters financially independent.

Inheriting the Kovac family fortune a few years later allowed Marisa to establish the foundation, cementing her position as lady bountiful.

But it wasn't until Sebastian Rollins arrived a couple of years later, that she achieved a goal far more elusive and important than money: social standing.

The marriage was an on-again, off-again situation, with them remaining friendly despite, or maybe because of, the time apart. Lily had no strong feelings either way about Sebastian. He was nice enough and he was good to Marisa, but he wasn't her father.

No one could replace her father, ever.

"I am sorry, Mom," she told her mother. "I'll make it up to you, I promise. But I've got to go. Sundays are always busy at the shelter."

Just as she keyed off the call, a text message came through from Ariel, her friend and shelter manager.

Can you come in early today? The storm drain's backed up at the shelter. We've been flooded!

COLD JANUARY RAIN sluiced across her windshield and her wiper blades beat a wap-wap-wap in their attempt to clear her field of vision.

The lot was overflowing with vehicles. The outdoor runs were full of dogs, huddling together under the meager shelter.

A line of people passed crates from one to another to be loaded into waiting cars, a bucket brigade of unhappy cats and kittens.

Lily ran past them into the building, then stopped short and looked down. The floor was covered with a good three inches of water. She continued inside, her feet squishing inside her sodden running shoes.

"Ariel?" she called.

She found her friend in the dog area, where the water was deeper still. A drain in the corner bubbled with murky-looking water.

"Thanks for coming in," Ariel replied, wiping dripping hair away from her face.

"What happened?"

Ariel paused and leaned on the broom she was using to sweep water out the door. "Time caught up with us." She sighed heavily. "The building has needed upgrades for years, but we kept putting it off. There's never enough money. The rain last night overwhelmed the plumbing system."

Then she smiled. "You probably want to see your new dog, right?"

"My new foster dog," Lily corrected. Ariel was determined to bring Lily into the tribe of dog owners.

"We'll see." Ariel led Lily to the outdoor dog run, where a single animal remained. "It's a good thing you signed up when you did. With the flood, we're desperate for foster homes."

The dog lay in the back of the chain-link run, his head on his paws, his eyes deep and soulful. And hopeless. He looked nothing like his photos now. He was bigger than she expected. Dirtier. Stinkier. Sadder.

"Oh, my," Lily said. "What's his name?"

"Valentine," Ariel replied. "He was a flea-market puppy, purchased last year as a Valentine's Day gift by a guy for his girlfriend. She dumped them both by spring, and Valentine's been bouncing around since then."

Lily raised her eyebrows. "He looks a bit like Marley, from the movie. Can't we call him that instead?"

"Sorry," Ariel said, not sounding sorry at all. "Every new owner has tried to change his name. It's the only one he knows. I think everyone expects him to be like the movie dog. Then they get him home and find out how energetic he is. He doesn't listen, they say. He destroys their furniture. They can't walk him. He runs away. He jumps on the kids."

Lily's heart ached. "And with each new home, he gets worse."

"Underneath that dirty, matted coat is an adorable personality just waiting to be released by the right person."

Lily and the dog surveyed each other. The tilt of his head and his half-cocked ears suggested that Ariel was right. It's just that there was so much of him. And so much mud.

"With some special TLC from you," Ariel said, "he'll be ready by our annual Adoption Option event in February."

"February." Lily bit the inside of her cheek. He needed so much. Would she be equal to the task? "That's a short time to undo a year of neglect. Keep in mind, I'm no Cesar Millan. I'm more… *See Spot Run*."

"You'll be fine," Ariel assured her. "A little basic obedience. You know, sit, down, off, heel, maybe a couple of tricks. Oh, and get him used to grooming. He enjoys rolling in stuff. A bath and a good brushing and he'll be gorgeous."

Not likely. But he had that heart-tugging quality in spades. "You haven't had much luck, have you, boy?" she murmured. "No one's ever even gotten to know you."

She knew what it was like to strike out, over and over again. And be overlooked.

He needed someone, badly, and she'd volunteered, after all. It would be fine, she told herself, as she tied up her hair and joined the rest of the cleanup crew.

Lily spent several hours transporting electronic equipment and files to Ariel's house. Someone brought in pumps to remove the lake of water standing in the concrete dog runs. Industrial fans hummed in every room. People from shelters in other municipalities arrived to take what animals they could.

But by the end of the day, it was clear that the building wouldn't be usable for some time.

Ariel grabbed a pile of towels and handed a couple to her. "Come on. Let's get Valentine so you can go home."

She unlatched the gate to the enclosure and beckoned to the bedraggled dog. "I'm so glad he's going to a nice home instead of another rescue center. He's already spent so much time in cages, with strangers. It's just not fair. He needs a break. Come here, boy."

Lily had taken in foster cats before, but a dog had always seemed like more commitment than she was ready for. This one seemed like more of a commitment than anyone was ready for.

She squatted down and made a clicking sound with her tongue. "Here, Valentine!"

The dog looked up, then bounded over as if he had no idea he was unwanted.

His tail swished muddy water against her legs as they dried him off, and he gave her hand a warm lick. He looked up at her with eyes that said he'd been cold and lonely for too long. Like he'd be delighted to be with her, like she was the best thing that had ever happened to him.

"We'll have a nice time together," she said.

Ariel scrubbed a towel over his tail until it fluffed out like a bottle brush. "It's only until someone applies to adopt him. Or you decide to adopt him yourself."

Lily laughed. "Good try."

"He'll need a little work." Ariel let the dog follow them down the empty hallway. "He never got much attention in his previous homes, so though he's sweet and friendly, he's not well socialized."

"I've got a park nearby," Lily said. "He'll meet lots of people and dogs there. That should help."

She was starting to get excited about the idea. She could do this. A little dog therapy, some unconditional adoration and fun were just what she needed.

Yes, she'd give this nice animal a break from a concrete cage, prepare him for his happy ever after, and get a little much-needed ego boost in return. Dogs were good for that.

And this one, with his liquid, pleading eyes, looked like he was just waiting to lavish someone with love.

Ariel clipped the leash onto the collar. "He needs practice leash walking."

"How bad can it be?" Lily reached for the leash, but Ariel moved past her.

"Let me."

As soon as Ariel tugged on the leash, the dog dug his heels in.

"Come on, boy," Ariel said.

She convinced him to take a few steps at a time until

they were near the door. The moment the dog saw the wide-open space behind it, he lunged forward, yanking Ariel behind him. Then began a dance, with the dog leaping and squirming like a fish on a hook, and Ariel trying to keep him from choking himself in his effort to escape.

"Whew!" Lily said, once he was safely installed behind the dog gate in the back of her mini SUV. "You weren't kidding about the leash walking. That will be priority number one."

"He's microchipped, in case he escapes," Ariel said.

"He won't get away from me," Lily replied with more confidence than she felt.

"He'll need lots of exercise," Ariel went on. "Consistent socialization with positive reinforcement. Car rides. Meeting new people. Meeting strange dogs. New places, sounds, smells. He's been confined and restricted so much that the world is a strange place for him."

"We'll begin as soon as we're settled at home," Lily assured her. "I'm looking forward to the challenge."

She was. A change is as good as a rest, isn't that what they said? She could do this.

"I'm sure it'll be fine." Ariel gave her a hopeful look. "Maybe the two of you will bond."

Lily laughed. "As soon as classes start up again in March, I won't have time for a dog. But he'll be great company for me while I'm free. And when our time is done, I'll go back to work and he'll be ready to make the right person fall madly in love with him. And at the end of next term, maybe I'll foster another dog."

Clear end-dates, no promises, nothing forever. One day, maybe, she'd find the right one and be ready to commit.

"Can't fault a girl for trying," Ariel said.

With her social life in the pits, her day job on hiatus and her mother's demands stressing her out, the dog would give Lily something positive to focus on, a reason to get up in the morning. She'd be doing a good deed, helping rehabilitate this poor creature.

Good for herself, good for the dog. Win-win.

Right?

Chapter Three

AN HOUR LATER, Lily was rethinking her decision. Her little house was filled with the smell of dirty, damp dog, and small clumps of fur were everywhere. Valentine needed a bath and a haircut, and the sooner the better. She'd planned it out in steps. First, she'd brush out the worst of the dirt and mats in the garage, to contain the mess. Then she'd take him for a run in the park. When he was good and tired, she'd give him a bath. Once he was dry, she'd use scissors to even out his coat.

It was a solid plan.

But when she'd brought him to the doorway of the garage and removed the ugly leather shelter collar, the dog had ducked out from under her hands and raced back into the house. A collarless dog that didn't want to be caught could be remarkably slippery.

"This is how it works, boy," she said, reaching for him. "You wear the pretty collar and leash—"

The second she got anywhere near his neck with the collar, he darted away. She should have left the ugly leather one in place, but how was she to know he'd react like this?

Walking a dog. It wasn't rocket science. People did it all

the time. But Valentine eyed the collar like it was spiked with poisonous darts. How could she train him to walk on a leash if she couldn't get a collar and leash on him in the first place?

"Come on, sweetie pie, there's a good doggie."

Liver treats were his weakness, she remembered. She got out the bag, crinkled it enticingly.

"See these?" She held one out, then dropped several onto the floor. While he crunched them, she quickly slipped on the collar, buckled it securely and clipped on the leash.

"Good boy, Valentine!" She patted him but as soon as he lifted his head, he realized the trap.

He took off down the hallway, dragging the leash out of her hand. As he rounded a corner, the leather strap caught on a small table, nearly upending an arrangement of dried hydrangea blossoms.

Lily caught it just in time. "Whew! That was a close one. I'm fond of those flowers, I'll have you know."

A crashing sound from the living room burst her momentary sense of triumph. She placed the vase—a piece of pottery she'd thrown and glazed herself—safely on the kitchen counter and ran to see the next catastrophe.

"Valentine?"

She looked at the room with dismay. An armless occasional chair was lying sideways next to the couch. The area rug beneath was partly flipped over and the floor-length drapes had been yanked askew.

A small whine came from behind the couch.

Lily righted the chair, moved it aside and hunkered down to peer behind the couch.

Valentine's dark eyes blinked back at her from the dim corner. He was panting, head down, angled away from the leash as if it was a snake.

He whined again and struggled backward but the leash was caught tight on the leg of the couch.

"Hang on, boy. I'll get you free."

Lily reached into the awkward space and freed the looped leather handle. Valentine fell backward, then scrambled to his feet but the leash he so desperately sought to escape followed behind him.

Lily had to laugh. It was that or cry.

As Valentine passed in front of her, she snagged the leash and hung on tight as the dog's feet slipped out from beneath him and he landed on his side.

"Oh, honey," Lily said, rushing to unclip the leash. "It's okay. That bad leash is off now."

The dog leaped up, planted both front paws on her shoulders and began licking her face, barking and whining his relief.

Lily fell against the couch laughing, helpless against the onslaught of affection. "Stop, Valentine, enough!"

Her house was a mess, her clothing was covered in dog fur and slobber, not to mention her face, but she hadn't laughed this hard in ages. It felt good. There was nothing like a dog to make you feel like a hero.

"Okay," she said, finally. "How about we take this outside?"

There was a word Valentine knew. He barked in delight and ran to the door. Lily sat on the steps of her cedar deck and watched as he ran circles in the small backyard, kicking up bits of grass. He was so full of joy, so completely uninhibited, it made her yearn to have some of that spirit. His fear of the leash forgotten, his loneliness in the shelter gone, his sadness at being left behind a thing of the past. He was simply, completely, in the moment, enjoying the fresh evening air, the freedom of a healthy, energetic body—

"Not the new shrubs," she cried as he plowed through her carefully mounded berm.

He stopped at her tone, all four feet planted in thick black composted bark mulch. Then he barked playfully and bowed low, sticking his wagging tail into the air, as if begging her to join him.

"Sorry, buddy," she said. "If you want to run with me, you're going to have to deal with the leash."

But he seemed to take her words as an invitation. He raced toward her and leaped up against her again, muddy paws, leaf-littered fur and all.

"Down, Valentine!" Lily angled away, hiding her head with her arms, but she might as well have been yelling into the wind.

And really, it had been a long time since she'd been the object of such unabashed and whole-hearted worship. She gave in and rolled onto her side, rubbing and patting him. He pawed at her and ever so gently mouthed her hands, whining his excitement. Then he flopped down beside her and rubbed his back up against her, groaning and moaning.

You, he seemed to be saying, *are the best thing that has ever happened to me.*

Don't get attached, Lily cautioned herself. She was keeping him temporarily, just until he found his forever home. He was her good deed, something to take her mind off her own loneliness, a creature to share her evenings with, a project to give her a sense of purpose and value.

She felt a pang of guilt. That was a lot to put on a poor dog. All the dog wanted was someone to love him. He had no idea that she wasn't in this for the long haul.

"There's someone out there for you," she murmured. "There's someone just waiting to find you. And when that happens, you'll never be sad or lonely or mistreated again."

A lump came into her throat. She'd never thought that at her age she'd still be searching for whatever it was that signaled the beginning of everything. Still searching for purpose and a sense of belonging.

Still searching for Mr. Right and happily ever after.

Maybe there was no such thing, despite watching as her friends seemed to be finding it, one after another, leaving her holding bridesmaid bouquets and smiling until her face hurt.

Valentine groaned again, and he nudged her arm to get her to stroke him again, his wavy tail slapping the cedar boards of the deck. She took the opportunity to clip the leash on again. He needed to get used to it. Regular positive reinforcement, right?

The dog's tail stopped wagging. His head drooped.

She'd betrayed him. He'd been so happy.

But he needed to understand who was in charge.

"Sorry, buddy. It's the way it has to be," she told him, her throat thick. "I'm not your person, but I'll wait with you until you find that person, okay? We'll keep each other company until then."

Maybe one day she'd be ready for a dog of her own. But until then, she'd do her best by Valentine. He deserved it. And her heart would be safe.

He followed her back inside.

"Should we go for that walk in the park now?" she said. She slipped on her jacket. The second she tugged on the collar, he lunged for the door, yanking Lily's arm nearly out of the socket, or so it felt.

"Whoa, hang on, Valentine!"

The leash slid through her fingers and the sparkly bits scratched at her palm. The dog threw himself at the door, leaping up against it.

"Take it down a notch," she said, hauling his bulk away from her reclaimed oak door. She didn't mind him adding more character to the distressed finish, but he looked like he wanted to tear right through it.

Once outside in the fresh air, in her new running outfit that just happened to match Valentine's leash and collar ensemble, he seemed to settle. They looked adorable together, if she said so herself. If you ignored his scruffy coat.

"Good evening, Mrs. Harley," she called to her next-door neighbor.

"Did you get a dog?" The older woman straightened up and peered over the laurel ledge that separated her yard from the sidewalk. There was alarm in her tone, the kind that suggested she feared for her azaleas.

"He's a foster," Lily explained. "I'm helping socialize him, so he can find his forever home. Would you like to meet him?"

She paused, and Valentine leaped up onto his back legs, clearly eager to meet a new friend.

"No, no, you go on." Mrs. Harley took a step back, making a shooing motion with her hands, trying to hide an expression of mild horror, as if she expected Valentine to burst through the laurels and devour her whole.

"He's very friendly," Lily said, using both arms to pull the dog back onto the sidewalk. He was certainly strong. His enthusiasm for new friends was admirable. Valentine did a flip and twist that ended with him on the wrong side, with the leash underneath his body.

"Hang on, sweetie," she said, squatting down to untangle him. He took the opportunity to lap his long, wet tongue across her face. "Ugh," she said with a laugh. "But I appreciate the sentiment."

She got him sorted and they continued their walk. Or rather, their drag. As in, he ran ahead, and dragged her along behind.

He was a lot stronger than she'd anticipated. A woman and little girl approached from the other direction. This sent a quiver of joy snaking up the leash, as Valentine thrust himself in their direction.

Lily pulled him off the sidewalk to let them pass.

"Is your dog choking?" asked the little girl. She pressed herself close to her mother.

"No," Lily answered, though the hacking bark certainly sounded like it. Valentine seemed intent on embracing the child and she hauled him away from them.

"Watch your dog!" snapped the mother. "He's out of control."

"Yeah, sorry about that." Lily felt her cheeks heat with embarrassment. "Valentine! Behave yourself."

Perhaps she should have chosen a less populated area for their first walk. It seemed like everyone had come out after work to enjoy the unseasonably dry weather.

There was a park a few blocks away that overlooked the river and had plenty of space to run. She crossed the street, pretending she didn't notice the drivers watching her with amusement, as Valentine alternately leaped at the end of the leash and attempted to wind himself around her legs.

He looked like a sugared-up preschooler on a search-and-destroy mission. Her excursion was turning into a walk of shame. Was there such a thing as Ritalin for dogs?

When they reached the riverside park and entered the wide expanse of grass and trees, Lily heaved a sigh of relief.

"Okay," she said. "Now there's no one to chase. We can walk nicely. Got it?"

The park was made up of acres of mostly wild space that

gradually sloped down toward the Fraser River. Great swaths of blackberry vines lined the edges, large oaks and mature vine maples provided shade in the summer and casual plantings of perennials and shrubs, with the occasional bench, appeared beside the path.

At the far end, beneath an old mission church, was a long-neglected cemetery. She liked to walk between the moss-covered stones, imagining the lives of the priests and nuns buried there so long ago. In the waning light, it was a magical place.

"You're named after a saint yourself," she told the dog.

Valentine glanced over his shoulder at her words, his lolling tongue long and pink and dripping.

"No pressure, though," she assured him. "You just be your loving self and we'll make sure you end up in a home that deserves you."

Just then, Valentine spied one of the little brown rabbits that populated the thick undergrowth. He gave a huge woof and lunged forward. By some miracle, Lily kept hold of the leash, but she stumbled onto her knees. Then the dog, no fool him, jumped sideways again and, to Lily's horror, twisted right out of his collar.

"Valentine!" she screamed.

She scrambled to her feet, her heart thudding in her chest, holding the empty leash and collar in her hand and saw the waving tail disappear around a patch of shrubbery. She called out again, but the dog was gone. There was nothing to do but run after him, following the path down the rain-dampened path and hope for the best.

"Valentine!" She shook her stinging palm and then took off after the mutt, who raced across a wide stretch of overgrown lawn, jaws agape, tongue lolling, eyes rolling white and wild, and disappeared over the ridge.

She ducked beneath a low-hanging cedar branch and felt a soft spray of droplets brush her face, the scent heady and green. Her sneakers slid sideways on the slippery grass and she nearly went down. How would she explain to Ariel that she'd lost her foster dog on the very first day? She couldn't be fired from a volunteer position, could she?

A biker rode past, grinning, and pointed over his shoulder. "He went thataway."

Lily gave him a thumbs-up, unable to speak. It would help if she knew the trail, but she rarely came out this far.

There!

She caught a glimpse of a shaggy tail heading toward the gentle slope leading down to the river, and redoubled her pace, her heart pounding.

"Valentine!" she yelled again.

Tangled thickets of blackberry vines cloaked the riverbank. If he got caught in the thorns, he could be hurt.

If he managed to get through them, she'd never catch him.

Her first day as a foster mom and already she'd failed.

Chapter Four

SHANE STOOD AT the entrance to the kitchen, his arms crossed, one hand under his chin.

Gram said she liked gray. Gray was in style, the girl at Home Depot said. He'd even gone on Pinterest and looked up paint colors. Gray was very in.

Now, with the thin evening light streaming through the big window over the sink into the room, it looked more blue than gray, but it would have to do. His shoulder was already screaming from the work. He wasn't about to do it again.

He was reaching for the ibuprofen bottle when a flash of something beyond the fence caught his eye.

Titan.

No.

He shook his head and downed the pills. Amazing how even after all this time, there were still moments when he'd forget that his dog was gone. Something random would trigger that instinctive expectation, that split second of being once again part of a team, of having his four-legged partner at his side.

And then the emptiness would return.

He rubbed his shoulder and went out onto the deck

where he could see the public parkland beyond. He'd seen something.

Yes, there it was. A loose dog, racing hell-for-leather over the rolling landscape.

Shane looked for an owner. No one to be seen.

He ran down the deck steps, across the yard and out the white picket gate into the park, aiming for the path the dog had taken. Who the hell had let their dog loose like this? The animal didn't look dangerous and there were no cars to worry about, but joggers and cyclists frequented the area, not to mention families with small children who might be frightened by a large dog.

Twenty yards ahead, the dog reappeared, rounding a clump of trees.

Shane put two fingers in his mouth and let out a piercing whistle.

The dog skidded to a stop, and glanced around comically, one ear up, one down, his ribs heaving in and out. Shane whistled again and the dog burst into flight, this time toward the source of the sound. Tongue lolling, lips flapping, he barreled straight at Shane, as if finding a long-lost friend.

"Atta boy, this way." Shane braced a palm against the trunk of the pine tree and tightened his leg muscles. The dog showed no aggression, only the hyper-manic joy of freedom, but he'd been knocked off his feet by dogs bigger than this one and even with full protective gear, it hurt.

After sidestepping the full-frontal assault, he hunkered down to his haunches, keeping his back against the tree for balance.

"Hey, buddy. Where's the fire, huh?" He held out a hand, hoping that the dog would come close enough for a collar grab.

No luck there. No collar, even if the dog would come close enough to touch.

The dog circled back, head down, tongue hanging out and dripping, lips drawn back in a subservient grin. But he stayed just out of reach.

Not much in the looks department. Mostly yellow Lab, with the elongated muzzle that suggested collie, and a heavier coat like that of a shepherd or husky, the look was at once generic, and unique in its many variances. He'd grown up with dogs like this in Prince George. They did well in the northern climate and often were good race dogs.

This specimen had a whole lot of thick, matted undercoat that needed to be combed out.

Shane pushed off the tree and began moving away, casually. "Here, boy." He snapped his fingers.

The dog whipped his head around at the sound and trotted after him. Shane ignored him. When the dog got close, he deliberately changed direction, moving away from him, slowing his pace, smiling to himself at the dog's obvious curiosity.

Finally, he stopped and squatted down. The dog lowered his head and body and came closer, almost crawling until he was at Shane's feet. He whined and rolled over onto his back, begging for a belly rub.

"Atta boy," Shane murmured. He patted and stroked and thumped the warm body as a rush of endorphins, triggered by the primal connection between human and canine, flooded through him.

This pathetic creature was underweight, with a filthy, matted coat. Nothing like Titan.

But that gangly adolescent awkwardness was the same, all feet and attitude and desperate to please.

A feminine shout came from the park side. The dog leaped to a safe distance again.

Shane peered up, shading his eyes, and saw the form attached to the voice, silhouetted against the sunlight.

A very nice silhouette. She came closer, her black jogging outfit revealing sleekly muscled calves, lean thighs, and just the right number of curves.

"Valentine!" Her voice was hoarse and frantic. "Here, boy."

Shane stepped out of the shadow of the tree. "I take it he's yours?"

She stopped short. Sun-kissed curls bounced on her shoulders. One hand went up to the zipper of her jacket. Pink. "Yes. No. Sort of." She held up a leash and collar. Also, pink. And sparkly. "He got away on me."

"So I see," Shane said. The dog, he noted, did not rush to greet the woman.

"Valentine, come," the woman commanded, adding a little foot stomp to the word. Frustration. Shane understood. Few things highlighted a person's impotence better than a dog that chose not to come when called.

"Maybe he doesn't like the name," he suggested.

"Don't blame me. He came with the name. I'm just fostering him. He'll probably get a new name when he's adopted." She pointed her index finger at the dog, her authority marred by the fact that she couldn't catch her breath. "Valentine, that's enough. Come."

The dog barked, play-bowed and danced away.

The woman darted after him and the game was on.

Shane knew it was wrong, but he allowed himself a few seconds to simply watch. She was easy on the eyes and her determined movements highly entertaining.

No way in hell she was catching the dog like that, but she seemed ignorant of the fact.

After a few minutes, he took pity on the woman. "He's loving this, you know."

She made a wild grab with both arms and the dog slipped away like a flag in the wind, barking, tail wagging, having the time of his life.

The woman turned, scowling and put her hands on her knees, breathing hard. Her hair danced in the breeze, tangled with bits of dead leaves or twigs from her run through the woods. Her eyes were the soft blue gray of an early spring sky. Wind swept. Storm tossed. Full of promise.

What would they look like if she smiled?

SHE BRACED ONE hand on the back of the bench. Valentine was on the opposite end, eyeing her. She feinted one way. He jumped, but didn't run, poised to see what she'd do next.

"He's loving this, you know." The man reached down to the canvas messenger bag lying on the bench and pulled out what appeared to be a paper lunch bag.

"That makes one of us." Lily grabbed for the dog, who danced just out of reach, then play-bowed, barked, and took off again. "Feel free to help. Or just stand there and watch. Up to you."

The man said nothing, but the hint of a smile played at the corners of his mouth. He was enjoying this as much as the dog was.

He took a few steps away and leaned casually against a tree trunk. He opened the paper bag, took something out and let the bag fall at his feet.

Lily glanced between him and the trash container, a few steps away. "Littering? Really?"

"Your dog's running loose in a public park." He took a large bite of his sandwich.

Valentine stood panting, possibly confused now that he was no longer the center of attention. He closed his mouth, lifted his head and sniffed the air.

"Tuna, left over from lunch," the man said, around his mouthful of food, giving her a knowing nod. "Irresistible."

"If you say so," Lily replied.

Valentine trotted over to the crumpled paper bag, nosed it.

"See?" the man said. "Hey, buddy. You like the smell of this, huh?"

"Good," Lily whispered, moving toward the dog. "You hold him and I'll—"

Valentine leaped away before she got anywhere close.

The man said nothing, but his lips tightened, and Lily got the distinct impression that he was annoyed.

"He was right there," she said. "Why didn't you grab him?"

He cleared his throat and turned toward her. "Ma'am," he said. "Your dog doesn't seem inclined to being grabbed."

Ma'am?

"I can't exactly leave him 'running loose' so if you have an alternative suggestion, I'm all ears."

The man bent down for the paper bag. He crumpled it loudly in his hand. Valentine's ears went up and he cocked his head.

The man tossed it at her. "Got any treats on you?"

Lily caught the crumpled bag, her annoyance growing. As it happened, in all the leash-and-collar kerfuffle with her new foster dog, she'd left them on the kitchen table. "I'm out. Would you like me to dispose of this for you?"

The man's eyebrows lifted and this time he didn't hide his grin. "Crinkle it. See how he's watching you? He likes the sound. And the smell."

And sure enough, Valentine was staring at her. Or rather, the paper bag.

The man broke off a piece of his sandwich and passed it

to her. "Give him this. You need to increase his food. And brush out those mats, or he'll get hot spots."

"Good to know." She ignored the dig.

"Hey, buddy, want some yummy tuna?" Lily squatted down and held out the bit of food.

The dog immediately trotted over, his scraggly tail sending pieces of dried grass and leaf litter flying.

"Give me the leash," said the man.

She passed it over. Valentine was nudging her for another bite of tuna sandwich and she obliged.

The man examined the collar, shook his head, unbuckled it, then making no sudden movements, approached the dog. He let Valentine sniff the dreaded item, then stroked and patted the dog, using the hand holding the collar. When he slipped it around the dog's neck and rebuckled it, it looked as simple as pie.

"No wonder he got away on you. The collar was way too loose." He adjusted it to fit correctly, while Valentine stood with head down and tail drooping.

"I kept it loose," Lily said, her words clipped and precise, "because he hates it."

"Maybe he hates it because of the screaming pink."

"Dogs are color blind."

"But they're not deaf." He clipped the leash onto the metal loop and handed it to Lily. "There you go. Your temporary Valentine, back where he belongs."

Lily took a step back. The man was quite tall. "Um, thanks."

He assessed her. Then he reached out and touched the side of her jaw. "You've got a scratch."

His eyes were gray and green with the odd fleck of brown. Beneath the dark stubble on either side of his mouth she could see lines that in a heavier man might be dimples. There were lines radiating from the corners of his eyes too. But those smile lines looked as if they hadn't been used in some time and the dark shadows haunting those strong bones spoke of long nights and too little sleep.

She put her hand to her face and forced herself to look away. "I must have done it when I was running through the woods. I'm sure it's nothing. Well. Thanks for…um…your help… See you."

She turned, tugged on the leash and this time Valentine trotted alongside willingly.

She barely saw the trail as she walked away, his searing gaze heavy on her back. Not until she got over the ridge and out of sight, did she pause and begin to breathe again.

"Our first walk," she said, looking at Valentine. "That was eventful."

He looked over his shoulder and whined. Already, the dog was more interested in a perfect stranger than he was in her.

"Sorry. You're stuck with me."

She touched her jaw again, letting her fingers drift down her throat. Such a small scratch, yet the sting sizzled all the way through her body.

She didn't even know his name.

Lily didn't stop for breath until she'd breached the ridge and knew for certain that the man could no longer see her.

She'd felt his eyes on her as she and Valentine had walked away. His disdain for her lack of knowledge was clear.

Okay, so she wasn't an expert. She had stuff to learn, as did Valentine. But they'd learn together. Even ignorant as she was, temporarily offering her home was better than letting the poor creature languish in a kennel for any more time, right?

As for a dog being a great way to meet people, well. Chalk that up to a big fail.

She'd met someone, all right. And yes, he was attractive enough. If you liked the irritable, unwashed look.

And he'd seen her in full panic mode, a mess, incompetence written all over her and twigs in her hair.

She lifted her free hand to touch the spot where his finger had landed so fleetingly. The brief point of contact still sizzled, setting off warning bells deep into her belly.

Not warnings of danger. Despite her reaction, he hadn't done anything remotely threatening.

He was just...annoyingly competent.

"Come on, buddy," she said to the dog. "We're almost home."

Lily walked back through the park to her own back gate. Valentine, now penitent at her side, kept his ears down, his tail at half-mast and his head drooping.

"I'm not the bad guy here," she said. "I'm rescuing you.

But dogs wear collars. It's the way the world works. You're going to have to accept it."

He gave her a white-eyed glance that told her just what he thought of that information.

She was simply going to have to work through it. He wouldn't get adopted until he could accept the leash and collar. Even then, with his behavior, it would be a challenge to find the right home. Or any home, for that matter.

Valentine cast a forlorn look over his shoulder, as if hoping to see the man again.

The man who'd had such a gentle touch, who'd mesmerized the dog with barely a word, who'd stopped him in his tracks and made him want to follow him.

As if he was some kind of dog whisperer himself.

Lily felt a twinge of jealousy. Valentine was supposed to adore her, not some stranger they'd run into on their walk.

No, she corrected. Valentine was not supposed to adore her. He was supposed to learn from her, become friends with her, and then happily move on to the people who'd become his forever family. The ones who'd fall in love with him thanks to the efforts Lily was putting in right now, to help him become a good companion.

It wasn't about her and her needs.

It was about helping a poor, neglected dog find a permanent home.

She had time and a home to offer, even if her knowledge of dog training was less than optimal.

Wasn't that enough? Ariel wasn't expecting miracles. All

she wanted was for Lily to get Valentine used to sleeping in a proper dog bed, coming when called and not chewing on socks and acting like a wild bull on steroids.

Except, he'd already left a path of destruction in her house. And his reaction to the leash had definitely been rodeo bullish.

Maybe she should look into finding a professional trainer.

No. She could do this. Just because some stranger made her feel inadequate, didn't mean that she wasn't up to the task. She'd get Valentine used to the leash, and then she'd head back to that park. If he happened to be there, he'd have a chance to eat his words.

"Okay, Valentine," she said as they entered the house. "Forget the bath for now. We've had enough excitement already, haven't we?"

The dog jumped up against her with his muddy paws and planted another big doggy kiss right on the cheek still warm from the stranger's touch.

Chapter Five

"So? How'd the first night go?" Harpreet asked.

Lily put her phone on speaker and went to the sliding kitchen door to let Valentine back inside the house. "Awesome."

In fact, the dog had refused to go to sleep in his crate. By the time she'd given up and let him loose in her bedroom, it was three in the morning and she was exhausted. She'd awakened at seven to his big paws digging into the small of her back. Paws that left dusty smears on her white eyelet duvet cover.

"Today, I'm giving him a bath," she added.

"Manny and I are going to Whistler for a week. We're going to go skiing, ride the gondola, watch bears, sit in the hot tub and drink wine. You're spending your break alone, cleaning up after a stray dog. There's something deeply wrong with that, my friend."

Three hours later, sitting in the laundry room in a lake of soapy water, she admitted that Harp had a point.

Oh, the dog was clean. She'd shampooed him with special stuff she'd purchased from the vet; she'd lathered, rinsed and repeated.

Twice.

The first time she'd completed the task, she let him outside while he was still wet. He'd promptly rubbed his face into the lawn, rolled, then remuddied himself digging a hole at the fence line, where if he was successful, he'd end up in Mrs. Harley's flower bed.

"Fool me once," she told the dog, who lay inside his crate, recovering from his second bath. His head rested on his front paws, his eyes down, as if he knew he was in trouble. "Next, drying and styling."

But that heavy fur didn't dry easily. As soon as he shook, it poofed out in pointy tufts that somehow stayed sodden at the skin level. The blow-dryer made him crazy, snapping and biting at the warm air until she gave up and turned it off.

So Lily clipped Valentine's leash to the collar and headed outside. The air was cool but sweet and misty as the sun broke through the clouds. A walk in the park would help dry that coat, and be good practice for him, too.

"What a good boy!" she said, as they started down the sidewalk to the park. "Are you tuckered out from the bath?"

As soon as they passed into the gently sloping expanse of rolling hillside in Heritage Valley Park, Lily picked up the pace. Valentine was doing so well, hardly fighting the leash at all.

She couldn't help but glance around her, wondering if the man from yesterday would be here again. She deliberately followed the path that went to the benches overlooking the river, in case that was a regular lunch spot for him.

Wouldn't he be surprised to see so much improvement in such a short time?

But the tall stranger was nowhere to be seen.

She made a couple of loops around the area, hoping it would be enough to fully dry his coat. Valentine only made two major lunges, both times after a rabbit. Lily's hold on the leash never wavered. She'd learned.

She reached down to pat Valentine. "You're a good boy, aren't you?" His coat felt even heavier now, fluffy on top but thick and dense beneath. It was going to be hard to comb through.

The dog glanced up at her, his eyebrows torqued, that big sweep of tail waving gently, and he whined.

"What?" Lily said. "He's not here."

They walked the three blocks back to her own restored bungalow and she led Valentine to the detached garage. She wondered if the man lived nearby. Maybe they were neighbors.

Maybe she should have introduced herself.

"Maybe you should stop thinking about him," she muttered.

She'd set up an old dinette table as a grooming station, covering the top with winter floor mats from her car, for traction. She pointed to the table.

"Jump up, Valentine."

Valentine cocked his head and whined.

"Jump." This time she patted the surface.

Again, the dog looked at her in confusion.

"Fine." Lily squatted down and hefted the dog's front end onto the table. "Up. We. Go."

But Valentine's back end didn't follow the front end. In fact, both ends did another twisty dance that ended with the table on its side, Lily on her back and the dog standing over her, licking her cheeks.

"Okay, we don't like the table. I can live with that." She got to her feet. "How about we both stand on the floor, while I brush you. Do you think you can manage that?"

He wagged his tail and gave her a woof.

"Right on, dude! But first, some tunes."

Lily put some music on her phone and sent it to the speakers in her garage. Luke Bryan sang about how most people were good, which was what she liked to believe. She put her hands up and danced along. Valentine put up his snout and howled.

They danced and howled until she heard someone pounding on the door. She fumbled for the mute button on her phone. In the sudden silence, the voice rang out loud and unmistakable.

"Lily, what on earth is going on in there?"

Immediately Valentine barked and ran for the door, leaping at it as if trying to see out the small mullioned window.

Oh, God.

"Mom?" She opened the door a crack, holding Valentine back with her leg. "It's pretty messy in here. You might not want to come in."

Marisa peered inside, clutching the edges of her cream

wool car coat. "Good heavens. Is that a dog?"

"Yes, Mother."

"But…why?"

Lily rolled her eyes. "Why is it a dog?"

"Why is it here?"

As Marisa seemed intent on entering, Lily took a firm grip on Valentine's collar and opened the door. "I'm looking after him for the shelter."

The dog yelped and squirmed, but Lily held fast.

Marisa came in, edging around Valentine and looked at the state of the garage. "Really, Lily, if things are so tight that you've resorted to buying your furniture at yard sales—"

"It was an estate sale and for your information, this aqua blue and chrome style is very on trend right now." She nudged the table out of the way. "Plus, I love it. Love doesn't always come with conditions, you know."

It was a dig, but she was tired of justifying her choices. The pleasure of color or form or texture, that gut-warm knowledge that this, yes this, worked, is what she went after when designing a living space. Whether her project was a college dorm room, an office lunchroom or a luxury condo, she relied on that instinct to direct her choices. Not the glossy full-page photos in expensive magazines. Or what some art critic decided was the epitome of desirable this week.

"Just because I object to you wasting your God-given talents," Marisa said, "doesn't mean I don't love you."

"How am I wasting my talents?"

"You know. Teaching at that little school." She sniffed. "If you worked for the foundation full time, think of what you could accomplish. Besides, how do you expect to meet someone when you spend your time rearranging furniture?"

"Mom." Lily took a deep breath. "Interior design is about far more than rearranging furniture."

"So you've said."

"And," Lily added, "if and when the right person comes along, I'll know. You're desperate. Not me. I'm fine."

"For now, but you're not getting any younger. Anyway. I'm not here to argue with you." She held out a pair of white envelopes embossed with the Kovac Foundation logo. "Your tickets to Saturday's dinner."

"Mom. I already told you I'm not going."

"You most certainly are." Marisa turned stern eyes her way. "We have a reputation to maintain, Lily."

"If it's just family, who cares?"

Marisa's lips tightened. "All right, there will be a few close friends attending as well. All the more important that you be there, and on your best behavior."

"It's not a scheduled foundation event, Mom. I have a life." Valentine broke free of the hated collar and leaped toward Marisa. "As you can see, I've got my hands full."

"If you wanted more volunteer work," Marisa said, lifting her hands out of the way of the curious dog's nose, "I know many excellent causes. There's no need for you to get yourself covered in dog hair and...mess."

"Valentine!" Lily lunged for the collar. Missed. "I like

looking after animals, Mom."

"If it's a question of a dinner date—"

"Mom. I told you. I'm busy." The dog disappeared around a pile of boxes.

"Chad is willing to give you another chance." She blinked mascara-heavy eyelashes, as if unaware of how her words would affect her daughter.

"How nice of him."

"He's a lovely man, from a wonderful family." Marisa seemed oblivious to Lily's tone.

"His last name could be Vanderbilt-freaking-Disney, and it wouldn't matter. I'm not interested."

Valentine reappeared, covered in cobwebs. He approached and began sniffing around the hem of Marisa's coat.

"No need to be crude." Marisa's smooth, stylish bob shuddered delicately. Her nostrils flared. "My Lord. What is that smell?"

"Wet dog. Possibly a dead mouse." Lily pulled him away and he reacted as he had before, veering back and nearly pulling her over. "Was there anything else, Mom? I've got a lot to do."

Marisa slapped the tickets onto the windowsill, pulled open the door and turned for a last, dramatic word. But whatever she was about to say didn't make it out as Valentine saw his chance. He leaped for the door, knocking Marisa off her Ferragamo pumps and right into the recycling bins.

Marisa shrieked.

"Mom!" Lily reached for her mother, just as the dog disappeared around the corner, to the yard where Marisa had no doubt left the gate wide open.

"Valentine!"

"Lily Andromeda Garner!" Marisa yelled, losing her cultured, dulcet tones. In times of extreme agitation, the lovely Marisa Kovac Garner Rollins became unrecognizable. Her roots showed, in more ways than one.

But Lily didn't have time to worry about her mother.

Right now, thanks to Marisa's obsessive thoughtlessness, Lily's good deed, her act of kindness, her one truly unselfish gift was going to end in disaster, if not tragedy.

SHANE BALANCED ON the ladder and reached out for the small seedling that had taken root in the gutter above the back door. In a house this size, there was no shortage of seasonal tasks and this should have been done months ago. Maintenance itself was a never-ending job, let alone taking on a renovation. No wonder the place had fallen into disrepair. Gram should have moved out years ago.

He missed, reached again, caught it and gave a big yank. The seedling, however, was rooted more deeply than he expected. The ladder wobbled as he tugged again, and he leaned back to redistribute his weight.

Gram had made him promise not to do any dangerous tasks while he was alone. As it was, she leaned over the kitchen sink watching through the window, cell phone in her hands.

"I've dialed nine one," she called, showing him the screen. The numbers were in a font size that was probably visible from space.

"I'm good, Gram. No need for paramedics."

The seedling came free, sending a little shower of debris down onto the deck.

"Don't come out until I've cleaned it up, okay?"

Instead, she opened the screen door and peered up at him, oblivious to the impact of the door against the ladder.

"What was that, honey?"

Shane grabbed the downspout and slid down the last three rungs of the ladder, landing on his feet just as it crashed down into the dormant perennial bed below.

"Never mind," he said. "That's it for death-defying jobs today. You don't need to stand guard. Though I appreciate the sentiment. And the butter tarts."

"If you're sure. There's a tae kwon do class starting soon." She glanced at the time on her phone.

"I'll be fine."

Suddenly, from the quiet street out front came a squeal of rubber and the sound of a car horn being honked by an irate driver.

Shane put down the broom and jogged around the side of the house to see if anyone was hurt. He found a man shouting angrily at something hidden behind his open car door.

"Is anyone hurt?" Not a kid, Shane hoped. Please, not a kid.

The park entrance lay at the end of the cul-de-sac and in nice weather, children ran in and out all day with their balls and bikes, their laughter part of the background neighborhood noise.

"Stupid dog," the man said, pointing. "Ran right in front of me!"

At Shane's voice, the dog's head appeared around the front of the vehicle, his ears perked forward, tail wagging wildly.

"Valentine?" He looked like he'd fallen into a vat of glue.

Gram came up behind him, squinting.

"What's going on? What's wrong with that goat?"

She'd gone her whole life without glasses and refused to admit defeat now.

The dog exploded toward them as if they were long-lost relatives.

Gram planted her legs and crossed her arms. No goat was going to bowl her over.

Shane stepped in front of her. "Whoa, there, buddy." He lifted a knee just enough to block the dog's chest.

Valentine gave a big ooof, then sat back on his haunches, hind legs splayed. His lips pulled back in a goofy doggy grin.

"Do you know this creature?" Gram asked.

"We've met," Shane said. At least this time, the dog wore a collar. He looked down the street. Where was the pretty handler in charge of this one-dog disaster area?

"Want me to call animal control?" The driver's annoyance had turned to concern. "He shouldn't be running loose. He's going to get hurt."

"I'll look after him," Shane said. "I'm sure the owner will be along any minute."

He hoped. This time, he'd get her name.

"You're not bringing him into my house," Gram said. "He looks contagious."

"I'll keep him in the yard, don't worry." Shane snapped his fingers and walked quickly toward Gram's sunny, grapevine-bordered garden, hoping the dog would respond as he'd done before.

No hesitation at all, this time.

Once they were through the gate, Shane latched it securely.

"He's panting," Gram said. "That's a sign of rabies, you know."

"He's not rabid." He thought of the box of dog supplies in the garage. The bedding, washed and folded. Clean dishes, neatly stacked. Well-used toys. Leashes. Collars. "Is there a saucepan I can use as a water dish?"

Gram gave him a narrow-eyed look that told him she didn't require twenty-twenty vision to see around his request.

"A saucepan, huh?" She shook her head and went inside to find one.

Shane turned back to the dog. His coat was tufted and spiky, the thick undercoat clumped and matted and smelling of coconut. "What has she done to you?"

Valentine gave a deep-throated woof. He turned his shaggy head, then ran to the picket fence overlooking the park and planted both front paws on the planks.

"Valentine?"

Shane recognized her voice immediately.

The dog barked and scratched at the fence and then her face appeared above the gate. This time, her blonde curls were caught up in a messy bun of some kind and she wore an old Kwantlen college sweatshirt with bleach stains on it. No jacket. She must be freezing.

"Oh!" The pink that bloomed in her cheeks was natural, like a sunrise, a mixture of embarrassment and apology. "Not again."

"Hello to you, too." Shane opened the gate and gestured for her to enter. "How are things going with your new dog?"

"Couldn't be better, as you can see." She gave a huff of annoyance, and instead of entering, held out the sparkly leash. "Would you mind?"

Valentine whined and dropped his head. Shane followed the dog's gaze. In her other hand, the woman held a pink brush.

"Ah," Shane said.

"Ah, what?"

He nodded toward the dog, hunched and cowering. "The whole finger-in-the-electrical-outlet look over there. Let me guess. You gave him a bath."

"Twice. And by the looks of it, I'll be doing it a third time. Valentine, come here. Right now."

The dog turned his head, every line of his body spelling out horror, shame and dread.

"He really knows how to milk it, doesn't he?" Shane said. "I take it he's not a fan."

"Doesn't matter. I'm going to brush out that coat, whether he likes it or not. I've got enough dog hair in my house to build a new dog." She pursed her lips again. "But first, I've got to get him home."

"And replace your fence. May I suggest chain link?"

At the look of horror on her face, he couldn't help but smile. "Kidding. It would ruin the neighborhood."

"We agree on that." She shuddered. "No, my yard is secure. My mother, however, is not. She left the gate open."

Perhaps it was the warm sunshine, or the fact that they were chatting over the fence like old friends, or maybe it was Gram, watching avidly through the patio doors. But the woman smiled and held out her hand.

"I'm Lily. Lily Garner. That's Valentine, as you already know. Sorry about this. I hope he didn't hurt anyone."

"Shane Bowman." Her grip was warm and firm, and that smile was every bit as appealing as he'd imagined. "A mild altercation near the park entrance, but no damage."

One side of that lush mouth went sideways, making a dimple appear in the cheek. "Thank you so much for catching him. Again," she added. "Any new tips for me today?"

"Just one." He gestured for her to hand him the brush. "If you were planning to use this on him," he said, tossing it into the trash bin, "let me stop you right there."

Chapter Six

THAT SHANE HAD a lot of nerve.

"That's a perfectly good brush!" Lily protested.

"Not for his coat."

It was tough to argue, given that her attempts at grooming had only made Valentine look worse. He was slipperier than an eel when wet and keeping hold of him while working took more strength and agility than she'd expected.

"And how much shampoo did you use?" He wrinkled his nose.

"Lots. He was filthy." She shuddered. "And rank."

"To you. Not to him." Shane sighed. "You see how he's rubbing his face on the grass? The poor guy's just trying to outrun his own stink."

She thought of the way she'd felt at her mother's Christmas fund-raiser, with the overly bright crimson and gold decorations. Dogs relied on smell the way humans relied on sight, which meant that she'd done to him what Marisa's decor had done to all those guests, only about a thousand times worse.

Was there nothing she could do right with this dog? And why did Shane happen to be there every time Valentine was at his worst?

"Fine. I'll rinse him again, as soon as I recover from the first two baths."

And grow another pair of arms. How did professional groomers do it?

"Hello!"

Lily looked up to see a gray-haired woman waving from the deck. She wore white coveralls and carried a can in one hand, a paintbrush in the other.

"It's the perfect time for a break," she said. "Shane, why don't you invite your friend inside for tea."

Shane closed his eyes momentarily, then waved a hand between them. "Lily, my grandmother. Gram, Lily."

"Dorothy Bowman, but you can call me Dolly." She walked onto the deck and stood at the rail.

"Pleased to meet you, Dolly. I'm Lily Garner. That bad boy is Valentine." The dog's ears lowered at the sound of the 'b' word. "I'm fostering him right now. I'm not doing a very good job of it, I'm afraid."

"Yes, Shane mentioned him. Valentine this, Valentine that. I was beginning to wonder." Dolly's face crinkled into a mischievous grin. "Now I understand."

A flash of ruddy color came into Shane's cheeks. "My grandmother exaggerates. It's an early sign of dementia."

Lily gaped but Dolly just laughed. "The only sign of dementia was getting him to oversee the renovation." She turned around and pointed to the door leading into what appeared to be the kitchen, in a state of disarray. "Does that paint look blue to you?"

"It's gray," Shane said. "They told me so at the hardware store."

"I'm myopic, not blind." Dolly lifted the paintbrush. "What do you say, Lily?"

"Blue," she confirmed.

Shane rolled his eyes. "Okay, so it's blue. What's wrong with that? It's still a nice color, right?"

"We agreed on gray," Dolly said. "Take her with you to the paint store, Shane. We need someone who knows what she's doing. I've got to go. Can't keep my cute tae kwon do master waiting. Nice to meet you, Lily. Hope we see much more of you."

His grandmother waved gaily to them and the screen door slammed shut behind her.

"Sorry about that." Shane's face was red, and he carefully made no eye contact with her. "Gram's mission in life is to get me married off. You happened to be in the line of fire."

Lily smiled, feeling a wave of kindred sympathy. "I could tell her I'm married with thirteen kids."

"Are you?"

His question carried no undercurrent and she found it refreshing.

"No. To both. As my mother reminds me every chance she gets."

He rolled his eyes. "Then you feel my pain." He eyed her sideways. "She means well. She's actually pretty cool."

"She seems nice." Lily'd always wished she had a grandmother like that, or a mother like that, for that matter. An earthy, kind person who let her hair go gray and made delicious-smelling soup and wore crystals and didn't criticize.

She found his embarrassment amusing but took pity on him. "Relax. My mom sets me up all the time. I decided that the last one was in fact the very last one. Next time I date someone, it'll be my choice. If I die single, so be it."

"Gram's threatening to get me on *The Bachelorette*."

Lily laughed. "Do it! I'd watch that."

He made a face. "She's just crazy enough to be serious. Speaking of crazy, do I really have to repaint the whole kitchen?"

"I think you do. She doesn't look like a woman you want to cross."

"You think you can pick a better color?"

Lily smiled. "Trust me. I do this for a living."

Mr. Dog Expert wasn't the only one who knew stuff.

"Really?" Shane's eyes lit up. The hunted look disappeared.

"Color and lighting can make the difference between a living space that's welcoming and comfortable and one that's cold and sterile. Gray tones are tough but I'm sure we can find the right one that will make your grandmother happy. It's a beautiful house. It's worth taking a little extra time to make sure you get it exactly right."

She was pleased to see that the coffered ceiling in the dining room was flat white. A line of paint indicated that he was continuing the same white throughout the main floor ceiling. It would look lovely, against the gray she had in mind.

The thought of doing hands-on work again instead of just teaching, excited her. "I can even get you my designer discount," she said.

"Even better." He looked at Valentine. "Maybe we could help each other out. I can hold him while you hose him down. When we're done with him, we'll hit your paint store. What do you think?"

"I love it. Your place or mine?" She groaned, hearing her own words. "Ignore the cheeseball line. And the question. Your grandmother wouldn't appreciate a wet dog running through her house. I've got a grooming area set up in my garage. You take Valentine and I'll lead the way."

"You must be cold," Shane said. He grabbed a heavy flannel shirt off the hook by the door and slipped it over her shoulders.

It smelled of sawdust. She closed her eyes for a moment as the scent reached inside and tugged memories of her childhood to the forefront. Then she opened her eyes. It was just sawdust.

Shane turned to the dog, giving her an excellent opportunity to evaluate the back of him, which she found rather pleasing.

She didn't want to be pleased. At least, not this pleased. She didn't want to think about men for a while. Not even well-mannered strangers who bantered with their grandmothers.

She tried to imagine joking like that with Marisa. Failed.

"Come on, buddy," he coaxed the dog. "Good boy, Valentine."

He spoke gently, his movements slow and sure. Valentine followed him like a kid heading for the candy store.

They walked through the park, rather than via the street.

"You might be on to something," he said, after a few minutes.

"Yeah?" she said. "What?"

"That cheeseball line." He looked sideways at her. "We both have pushy families. Maybe, if… Never mind."

"Wait." She stopped walking. "You mean, we could pretend to be involved with each other, so my meddling mom and your meddling grandmother would stop matchmaking. Or, in your case, engineering your meteoric rise to television fame."

Shane put up a hand. "It's ridiculous. Forget I said anything."

"Nuts," she agreed. "Totally insane."

"We'd have to be completely desperate."

"Which we aren't."

"Of course not."

Who was this guy? And why had Valentine thrown them together not once, but twice?

Her heart fluttered again, imagining the two of them painting Dolly's house. Just wait until she told Harp and Dani. They'd be overjoyed to learn that she was dipping her toes back into hands-on work. They wanted to start a three-person design firm, but she couldn't even consider that until Sara came back to the foundation.

Maybe not even then.

Those that can, do. Those that can't, teach.

Or work for their mothers.

What if she and Shane did pretend to be dating?

She knew immediately what conclusions her happily-ever-after-oriented friends would jump to. Could she convince them that this was simply a mutually beneficial situation that had nothing to do with attraction?

Because this wasn't about attraction, she reminded herself, letting her gaze run down his long, lean form. He did good things to a pair of jeans. And those shoulders were perfect.

Excellent facial symmetry, too.

Very, very nice.

She told herself she was simply admiring him from an aesthetic point of view. Nothing wrong with that, right? After all, like she'd told him, it's what she did.

Harp and Dani would never believe that she wasn't interested.

She wasn't, though, she told herself sternly.

But damn, look at the man.

No, she wasn't going to tell anyone about Shane.

Was she?

Of course not!

There was nothing to tell.

But as they walked past Mrs. Harley's front yard, the old

lady straightened up from her winter pruning and, behind Shane's back, gave Lily two thumbs up.

If everyone was going to make assumptions anyway, maybe they should go along with it.

Since it was just for show.

LILY'S HOUSE WAS less than half the size of Gram's place and considerably newer. Built in the fifties or sixties, Shane guessed, from the size of the rooms. The bathroom where they'd rinsed Valentine barely fit the three of them and in fact, Lily had finally stepped right inside the tub, so she could maneuver the handheld shower without soaking the entire room.

It had felt too intimate, given their brief acquaintance.

He wished he hadn't made the ridiculous suggestion about them dating out loud. Lack of sleep and Gram's relentless nagging was taking a toll.

Lily probably thought he was a lunatic.

They barely knew each other yet she seemed to understand his situation.

He tried not to look like he was snooping but couldn't help noticing little things about her.

She hung her towels in descending order beside the sink, used a purple toothbrush and had a sticker saying 'You've Got This!' on her mirror.

She didn't know much about canine behavior but had a

big heart and the kind of internal brightness that drew people to her the minute they saw her.

So how was it possible that a woman like Lily had to suffer through unpleasant setups? She could have any man on the planet.

If her house was anything to go by, she was very, very good at her job. He didn't know colors. To him, her walls were beige, but not the boring beige of every house he'd ever lived in. When he walked into her house, he felt...embraced. Welcomed.

At home.

She didn't crowd the place with knickknacks and all the items she displayed appeared to have a purpose. The desk in the corner held an antique letter opener, a brass globe, and a tall hurricane lamp. He bet that when the power went out, she used that lamp.

In the living room, she had simple, solid furniture, a thick soft area rug and a couch that looked like it was meant for napping.

By the time he'd escaped the damp confines of Lily's bathroom, he'd also felt her curls against his cheek as she bent over the dog. He'd seen the outline of her breasts and the gleam of perspiration on the tan skin of her neck. He'd heard her laugh when the dog shook, splattering them both.

Despite the elegant comfort of her home, she didn't freak out when Valentine ran down the hall, dripping water all over the polished hardwood.

She'd only laughed more and gone after him with a towel.

She'd created a cozy haven for herself, a place of comfort, but Lily's real gift was she'd also made it comfortable and welcoming to others.

Back it up, dude. You don't know her. You're helping with the dog and she's giving you some free decorating advice.

That's it.

LILY STOOD IN the garage and shoved a hank of wet hair behind her ears. She knew she looked a mess, but Shane was also rumpled from their adventures in dog bathing. It was way easier with someone holding the rambunctious animal. The shampoo smell wasn't as strong now, and she hoped it was less offensive to Valentine.

Shane beckoned the now clean and dry dog to his side, then dropped to his haunches and ran both palms down the animal's rib cage. He nodded at her to do the same.

"Feel that?"

It felt like layers of damp cotton batting lay beneath the top fluff. "Are those mats?" Long coarse hair clung to her hands. She wiped them on her jeans, which only spread the hair around.

"That's why I brought these along." He held a set of black hair clippers. "This is the only way you're going to get rid of those. I had a feeling we'd need them."

"You just happened to have a pair lying around?"

He bent down and plugged the device into the electrical outlet. His voice was muffled. "I did."

"You're not just a dog whisperer but a grooming expert, also?"

He made a sound that wasn't quite a laugh. "Nope. Just a guy with random knowledge, happy to share it."

But there was something sad about the way he said it, as if he considered it not only random, but also trivial and of no value.

"Well, lucky for me." Lily held the dog's head as Shane got started. "Stay still, Valentine. This won't take long."

The dog, perhaps exhausted after his third bath of the day, stood motionless. The buzz buzz of the clippers soon took on a soothing drone as layer after layer of heavy fur fell away from the dog. Shane worked quickly, to her relief. She was grateful for his help but wished she didn't need it. She'd volunteered to care for Valentine on her own.

At least she'd be able to repay him with paint color advice.

Suddenly the dog flinched.

"It's okay, buddy," Shane said. "Inside the flank is always a sensitive spot. Very easy to cut that loose bit of thin skin." Then he paused. "Oh. Damn."

Lily craned her head to see what he'd noticed, but his broad back was in the way. "What's the matter? Did you cut him?"

She could feel the dog's fear growing as he trembled beneath her hands.

"No," Shane said quietly. "Look."

He pointed.

Lily's breath caught in her throat. Beneath the creamy fuzz that was left after the matts had been shaved off, was a faded pink scar, star shaped and shiny in the center.

"Oh, my God." She met Shane's eyes, saw her concern mirrored in them. "What do you think happened?"

Shane shook his head. "Hard to say. It's an old injury, and it didn't heal well. See the puckering?"

Shane clipped away more fur, and Lily watched closer now. They found another scar, similar but smaller, on his rib cage, and a thinner linear scar on his back leg.

"Poor Valentine." Lily pressed a kiss to the top of his furry head. "Who hurt you?"

"Pups get into all sorts of things," Shane said, keeping his eyes on his work. "He's an active dog, loves the outdoors. Could be accidental, running into a broken branch, scraping against a piece of metal. A million possibilities."

"Ariel said he'd been tied up in a backyard at his last home."

Shane glanced up from his work. "How many homes has he had?"

She explained his background and why it was so important that he be properly prepared for his next home.

"He needs someone who'll love him for the rest of his life," she finished. "I'm going to make sure that happens."

Shane continued clipping, working his way up Valentine's body. "Oh, no," he said suddenly. He turned off the clippers. "Oh, man."

Lily looked at the freshly clipped area on Valentine's neck, where the hair growth was sparse, and the skin was rough and raised.

She felt her own throat close. "No wonder he hates the collar."

"I'm guessing he was tethered with a rope. Probably half-strangled himself trying to get free."

Lily shook her head, blinking hard, willing away the tears.

"I'm so sorry, Valentine." No wonder leash walking was a problem. The collar probably hurt him and brought back terrifying memories. And she'd been so adamant that he accept it. "I'll get you a harness, first thing in the morning."

"Not your fault," Shane said. "You couldn't have known."

His voice was gentle, but it only made her feel worse. "I should have been more patient. I should have tried to look at the problem from his perspective. It's just like the shampoo. It never occurred to me to think of what he was experiencing."

"Hey, hey," Shane said. He set down the clippers and took her hand in his. "You've opened your home to this dog. You're giving him a chance, even though you don't know a lot."

"I don't know anything," Lily wailed. "He needs way more help than I can give him. Ariel wants him ready for adoption by February. That sounded like a challenge yesterday. Now, it sounds impossible."

But she'd taken on this responsibility and she wouldn't turn her back on Valentine, especially now that she'd seen the effect of his earlier experiences.

The fact that he was such a good-natured dog, despite his situation, made her even more certain that he deserved the right home.

He still had her hand wrapped in both of his, holding it tight, stroking gently with his thumb. It should have felt strange, but it didn't. It felt right.

"I don't know if I can do this, Shane," she said.

His hazel eyes were filled with pain and she sensed a battle inside him. Then his expression eased. He squeezed her hand.

"I know you can."

Chapter Seven

Lily released Valentine into the yard and he took off like a shot, running in joyous circles, pausing to shake, then taking off again. Without the big, matted coat, he appeared smaller, thinner.

"He's got the body of a runner," Shane said. "Maybe he's got sighthound in his ancestry, somewhere. He'll need a home with regular exercise."

He had no business reassuring Lily. Valentine needed more than simple socialization and love; he needed remedial training by someone who knew what they were doing.

Which was not the woman in front of him, no matter how well intended she was, or how much affection she lavished on him, or how hard she worked.

"No wonder his previous homes didn't work out." Lily shook her head. "Look at him go."

"I've seen a lot of dogs like him, back home."

"Where's that?" Lily picked up a broom and began to sweep up the piles of dog fur.

He opened a garbage bag and helped stuff the fur deep inside. "North. In and around the Prince George area. We used to race them." He picked a big piece of fluff off her shoulder. "Sorry. You'll be finding this stuff everywhere for months."

She frowned. "I hope this doesn't sound rude, but isn't sled dog racing cruel?"

It wasn't the first time he'd heard it and it wouldn't be the last.

"You'd have to see it to understand, but the dogs love what they do. You can't win unless they're in top condition, so most dog men treat their animals well. But people are good and bad, wherever you go."

She leaned over a table to reach her broom into the corner. The bottom of her faded sweatshirt rose with the motion, exposing a creamy slice of skin. No tattoo. Nice.

She straightened up, caught him looking. "What brought you down here to the valley?"

He rolled his shoulder and stepped closer to the door. "Life, I guess you could say. How long is the paint store open?"

This was more conversation than he'd had with anyone in ages. Seeing Valentine's scars had already brought her down. No need to distress her more with his own sob story. At least, not all of it.

"We've got an hour," Lily said. "Would you mind if I took a quick shower? I'm covered in dog hair."

"Of course. I'll play with Val in the yard, make sure he's good and tired before we lock him up."

Lily's bathroom window looked out onto the backyard and even though the glass was frosted, Shane had to work hard not to glance up at it. He could imagine perfectly what she looked like, with her head tipped back, the sudsy water slipping over those creamy curves.

He and Tanya had been together for almost ten years. They'd been each other's firsts. And since Tanya, he hadn't had interest, let alone energy, for anything.

One woman.

No wonder the dating scene terrified him. Gram had no idea.

Or, maybe she did. Maybe she thought his story was exactly what the producers were looking for.

Damn. If he didn't get Gram off his back, he was gonna end up on reality TV, his twenty-eight-year-old almost-virgin status a dramatic secret revealed before the final commercial break.

He groaned.

He needed to get out there again. Or at least, make Gram think he was.

He glanced up at the bathroom window, behind which stood the only remotely eligible woman he'd spoken with in months, naked and dripping.

LILY TOOK ONE last minute under the pounding spray, sighing in pleasure as the aroma of wet dog disappeared down the drain. She was still shaken by the scars they'd found on Valentine. He'd been through more than she'd even guessed, which made it even more important that his next home be his last. He'd had too much pain and disappointment in his short life.

The next time someone took him home, she vowed, it would be for the rest of his life.

But he wouldn't find that home with his current behavior problems. Certainly not now that he looked like a skinned rat.

By February he'd be filled out, with a full coat again. Whether she'd been able to teach him proper doggy manners by then was another thing entirely.

Shane seemed to think she could do it.

She wished she had his confidence.

She scrubbed off and rinsed quickly, anxious to get to the paint store. She had some favorites in mind. She'd get some sample tins and they'd paint a bunch of patches to see which one worked best.

Suddenly she heard Valentine down the hallway, followed by a momentary scrabbling sound at the bathroom door.

The flimsy doorknob was no match for a determined dog, and the door crashed open, so hard that it bounced against the wall, sending her clean clothes sailing onto the floor.

"Valentine!" she shrieked, yanking the shower curtain against herself.

The dog raced into the tiny room, pounced on her clothing and grabbed her bra, the white one with yellow happy faces on it that always gave her spirits a lift.

With a look of pure evil genius, he shook it, and took off out of the room.

"No!" Lily wrapped herself in a towel and ran after him, trying not to slip on the wet floor. She had to get the bra back before Shane saw it.

She rounded the corner of the living room and saw Valentine waiting for her, his butt end in the air, the bra dangling from his mouth. If a dog could look calculating, that was the look on his face. A calculating, comedic thief of a dog, a badly groomed lovable pirate.

"Give me that." She held out one hand, edging closer, keeping a firm grip on the edges of her towel. "Give it to me. Right. Now."

The skinny tail wagged slowly.

"Valentine."

She took another step. The wagging accelerated and then with a muffled yelp he was off again, his prize still securely held.

A rush of cool air filled the room as Shane came in from the backyard.

"What's going on? I heard a scream."

He came around the corner, saw her and froze. "Oh."

"Yeah," Lily said, clutching the towel tighter. "The dog stole my bra."

"They love underwear," Shane said. "It's the smell."

She glared at him. "Excuse me?"

"I mean," Shane backpedaled, "your underwear has your

scent on them. That's what the dogs like. I didn't mean—"

"Stop, I beg you." Lily squeezed her eyes shut. "Can you just get it back, so I can get dressed? We can hash out the finer points of my embarrassment later."

Valentine took that moment to return. The bra was gone. But he'd managed to get back into the bathroom again because now, between his jaws, were the matching thong panties, also white with sunny-yellow happy faces.

"Cheery," Shane said, nodding approvingly.

Lily couldn't speak.

The dog pranced up to Shane and sat, as if he was the best dog in the entire world.

Shane reached into the pocket of his jeans and pulled out a treat. "Drop it," he told Valentine.

The dog looked at him.

Shane moved the treat closer. The dog backed up, uncertain as to the expectations and unwilling to part with his prize.

Shane moved the treat in front of him, giving the dog a good whiff of freeze-dried liver. "You want this? You have to drop it first."

Lily shivered as the air from outside brought goose bumps to her damp skin. She took a step closer to the dog, ready to retrieve her underwear the second they were free, but Shane held up a hand.

"No distractions, please."

She gritted her teeth and stepped back.

Shane put both hands toward the dog. One was palm up,

his fingers slightly curved, ready to catch the panties. The other higher, making Valentine look up and reach for it.

The dog made his decision. Shane snatched the scrap of fabric before it hit the floor and tucked it into a back pocket. "Good boy." He gave the dog his treat and then patted him roughly, making the animal wiggle with delight.

It made quite the image: Shane, squatting down beside the idiot dog, with her underwear poking out of his jeans like a flag.

"Do you mind?" She held out her hand.

At that moment, the front door opened and Marisa's head poked in.

"Lily, darling," she called out as she walked in. "Oh. Oh dear."

The dog, always ready to make a bad situation worse, ran into the kitchen and returned a split second later with more happy faces.

"Valentine! Drop it right now!" Lily commanded.

Ignoring her once more, he raced up to Shane and sat at his feet, the bra dangling from his jaws, awaiting his treat.

"Mother, what happened to knocking?"

"I tried. It seems you couldn't hear me." She glanced over the three of them. "Should I be alarmed?"

"Valentine got into the bathroom while I was having a shower and stole my clothes," she said, feeling the neon redness of her face warming the skin that only moments ago had been chilled.

"Whatever you say," Marisa said, lifting both palms up.

"I'm not judging." Her eyes slid to Shane, spent a moment on his back pocket, then went back up to his face. She held out her hand. "Marisa Rollins. Lily's mother."

Shane tugged the thong panties from his pocket and tossed them to Lily.

"Shane Bowman." He wiped his palm on his jeans and held it out. "Lily's...dog trainer."

"Dog trainer." Marisa gave him a limp handshake and then shook her fingers lightly. "You don't say."

"Mom, it's not what it looks like."

"I should hope not," she said.

"Or maybe it is." Shane lifted his eyebrows.

The dog whined. Shane exchanged the bra for a treat and the dog pranced to the couch, crunching loudly.

Marisa gave Shane a careful smile. "You seem to have your work cut out for you, Shane."

"He's a handful." Shane returned her gaze evenly. Lily tried not to watch him gently folding her bra into his big palm.

Marisa narrowed her gaze, as if in her book of people, she wasn't quite sure where to slot Shane. "So is my daughter."

"She must take after her mother."

Marisa's eyebrows went up. This time her smile was genuine, if confused.

Lily wasn't sure which one of them was worse. "Excuse me, if it's not too much trouble, I'd really prefer to continue this conversation with my clothes on."

"Please," Marisa said.

Shane's eyes met hers. They were full of humor but that shifted in an instant to something stronger, darker, hotter, sparking something vivid and alive and liquid inside her, deep down at the center of her being.

"If you insist," he murmured.

He leaned closer and when she reached for the bra, the side of his hand grazed hers. Warm, solid, a little rough, it added to the sizzle.

"I'll be right back." She fled to the safety of the bathroom. Inside, she leaned against the closed door.

Shane was flirting with her. There was no doubt about it. Lily wasn't sure what shocked her more: that he was being charming, or that his charm seemed to have at least a momentary positive effect on Marisa.

They weren't doing this. They'd agreed it was crazy. Yet there he'd stood, giving Marisa every reason to believe he wanted her.

And here she stood, with her underwear still warm from his touch, sizzling with unexpected desire.

Chapter Eight

TWO DAYS LATER, Lily and Valentine were on their way to the park again to meet with Shane for some lessons in basic obedience. Last night, they'd painted five different shades of gray on Dolly's walls, all of which Shane claimed were exactly like the color he'd already used.

She couldn't wait to see them now, in the light of day. She'd narrowed it down to her two favorites, Fog Mist and Cloudier. Dolly had talked about bringing some friends over to help them choose, but Lily agreed with Shane that the real reason was to introduce them to her.

Shane's new girlfriend. His Get Out of Jail Free card.

And her Get Out of Marisa's Blind Dates card.

Since the embarrassing underwear incident, Shane had reverted to his usual reticence, keeping the discussion focused strictly on business. Lily told herself she was relieved. She hadn't expected to feel such a confusing melee of emotions and was more than happy to put it all behind them.

Had she imagined the flirting? He'd made it clear that he was not looking for romance, no matter the heat in his eyes when he'd handed her the panties. Despite the sizzle he stirred in her belly, neither was she.

She wasn't used to the kind of casual, neighborly friendship they'd landed on. It was extraordinary, to her, for its comfort and simplicity, the honesty and lack of subterfuge, of agenda or games. She needed to accept it for what it was.

Valentine tugged against his harness, his head high, ears perked, nostrils quivering. Looking for Shane, Lily thought. Though the trees shimmered with the silvery-green of buds about to break, the air was crisp, and she was glad she'd worn her down-filled vest over her hoodie.

The dog gave a yelp and tugged harder.

Shane was sitting on a park bench overlooking the river but stood up when he saw them. He wore a fleece-lined denim jacket, faded black jeans and scuffed leather work boots. He was an attractive man, she admitted. In another life, in another time, if they'd met while they were each in a receptive frame of mind, she might have acted on that attraction.

"Good morning," she called. "Valentine, behave yourself."

The dog was beside himself with joy, crow hopping and turning circles.

Shane ignored the dog and fell into step beside Lily.

"Every time you give him attention when he misbehaves," Shane said, "you reinforce the negative behavior. Without consistency on your part, he'll never improve."

She stopped, stung by his tone. Then she thrust the leash at him, smacking his shoulder for emphasis. "Show me, smart guy."

Shane caught the leash, wincing, and transferred it to his left hand.

His right shoulder, she noticed, was higher than his left, tensed and rolled inward. Was he favoring that arm?

"Are you okay?"

"It's nothing." He increased his pace and took a sharp left, bumping the dog with his knee. Valentine yipped and scrambled out of the way.

"Hey! You almost stepped on him."

"He needs to watch my feet. This teaches him that."

He took another left and this time, Valentine stuck to his side and kept pace, so focused he didn't react to the cyclist passing by.

"You're in a grim mood today." She hesitated. "I appreciate what you're doing, but if you don't have time, I understand."

He gave his head a little shake. "Sorry. Didn't sleep well last night."

Between squirming with embarrassment and trying to figure out what, if anything, was happening between them, Lily hadn't slept much, either.

He adjusted his posture. "Let me start again. Positive training is all about motivation. Find out what an animal wants, then use that desire as a reward when they perform the behavior you're seeking from them."

He looked down at Valentine, who was staring intently at a group of kids with a ball.

"Valentine," he said, snapping his fingers.

The dog whipped his head back.

"Good boy." Shane tossed him a liver treat. "From now on, he works for everything. No free lunch, no free treats, no free patting or praise. All the cuddling and coddling you've been doing? No more."

"That's doesn't sound very positive to me. He needs kindness and affection. You saw the marks on him. You know how he's been treated."

Shane shook his head. "You won't undo that by indulging him. You don't have to be cruel, but you must earn his respect. Once he sees you as a kind of demigod, the giver of all good things, the sunshine of his life, he'll bend over backward to earn your praise."

"Easy for you to say." The dog sat at Shane's feet, looking up at him with a worshipful expression. It wasn't fair. She was the foster mom. She was the one who was supposed to be getting the doggy love.

"I don't give my affection easily." There was a strange undertone to his voice. "It means more then, when I do give it."

Something was different about Shane today and Lily wasn't sure what to make of it. There was an edge to him, something hard and sharp, like he was regretting the camaraderie of yesterday. Was he pulling away from her? Or was he trying to get her to pull away from him?

"He's basically like Helen Keller," Shane continued, "blind, deaf and dumb to what people want from him, but desperate to communicate. We use what drives him—liver treats, the desire to play—to our advantage."

He was articulate and passionate about his subject material.

"You're really good at this," she said. "I'm surprised you don't have a dog, yourself."

He froze. Except for a tendon that jerked in his neck, he stood completely still. She'd hit a nerve. You don't know anything about this man, she reminded herself.

Then he exhaled, and Lily also let out a breath she hadn't known she'd been holding.

"We'll do a few more exercises, then go to Gram's." He held the leash toward her. "Your turn."

She took it but when she moved forward, Valentine hesitated, looking back at Shane, clearly confused.

"Come on, boy," she said, patting her thigh. "You can do it."

He whined and followed, but his reluctance was evident.

"Be firm, Lily," Shane said. "Snap the leash. Demand his attention."

He instructed her like a drill sergeant. Walk straight, turn left, turn right, about-face, speed up, slow down. She tried to keep control, to walk briskly and give clear guidance, but Valentine still nearly tripped her several times.

"Use your voice, Lily. Talk to him. Whistle. Snap your fingers. Force him to pay attention and praise him when he looks at you."

"Easier said than done," she muttered. Then she lifted

her voice. "Come on, Valentine, that's a good boy, watch me!"

The dog's tail wagged but his heart wasn't in it.

"Tell him what you want, Lily," Shane instructed. "Make him listen. He wants to please you, but he doesn't know how."

"I'm trying!"

"Try harder."

She did a figure eight, tugging Valentine into position but he nearly got between her ankles.

"If he gets underfoot," Shane said, exasperated, "step on him."

She stopped, turned around and faced him. She'd had enough of his impatience. "If you don't want to be here, Shane, just tell me and I'll take him home. But don't yell at me."

"I'm not yelling!" He squeezed his eyes shut momentarily and then lowered his voice. "I'm not yelling."

Deep lines cut into the skin around his eyes and mouth. He held his right arm tight against his abdomen.

"And if you're in pain," she said, "for heaven's sake, say something. We don't need to do this now."

"I'm fine."

"Look at me," she said. She could be direct. She could give instructions.

He met her gaze. "What?"

She feinted in his direction. He jerked sideways and immediately grimaced, hunching over his right arm.

Lily exhaled. "Come on," she said. "We're done here."

"TOO MUCH PAINTING," Shane said, slipping off his jacket. His shoulder was throbbing. He'd been pushing too hard lately. The overhead work especially.

Damn it, he never expected rehab to be such a long, drawn-out process. He put in the effort. He did his part. He should be back to full strength by now.

"How late did you work last night?" Lily glanced upward. "You finished the whole ceiling? No wonder you're sore. You're lucky you can move your head at all."

"I wanted to get it over with. Gram can't list it until it's finished and I'm behind schedule."

Once Gram's house was completed, what would he do? Where would he go?

That's where his mind always came up blank.

Valentine, tired from the training session, collapsed on a pile of tarps next to the window and let out a huge sigh.

Lily turned in a circle, shaking her head at the blue-gray walls. "You should lie down."

Definitely. But not while she was here. "What do you think of the colors?"

"Tell Dolly it's between these two." She took a carpenter's pencil and circled the painted patches numbered two and five. "Either of them would work with the flooring and the cabinets."

"Got it." A couple of ibuprofens and a rest and he'd be good to go.

She put her hands on her hips. "Seriously, Shane. You look like you're going to pass out."

"Don't be dramatic." He rubbed the joint. He ought to make an appointment for more laser therapy. "It'll pass."

She pointed to the kitchen chair. "Sit."

From the corner, Valentine's head popped up.

She laughed. "Not you, Val."

The dog flopped his tail and went back to sleep. Despite her insistence that she was only fostering him, she cared for that dog. When the time came to let him go, she was in for a world of hurt.

But even if she kept him, it would still end, one way or another, sooner or later.

That was why he didn't have a dog. He'd never put himself through that kind of pain again. He and Titan should have had at least another five or six years together.

If Titan had obeyed him that night, maybe they would have.

"I see I haven't motivated you to obey me." Lily took him by the arm and pushed him toward the chair, a teasing smile on her face. "What do I have that would make you desperate to please me, I wonder?"

Yellow happy faces swam in front of his eyes. He shook them away, then winced at the movement.

He straddled the chair, folded his arms over the back and rested his chin on them. "I'm not a fan of liver treats."

She stood behind him and before he realized what was happening, her hands were on him, her fingers kneading into the knotted muscles.

He gasped. The worst of the damage was on the front of the joint, but compensation left the muscles and tendons across his back overworked. Whatever she was doing hurt like holy firewater, but he knew, from all the pain and torture of the last year, that it's what he needed.

"This isn't just from painting," Lily said quietly. "What happened to you, Shane?"

THERE WAS A knot the size of an egg in the broad muscles across the right side of Shane's upper back. It was hot and rock-hard under her palms.

"Take off your shirt," she instructed.

"What?" He arched away from her. "No."

"Oh, come on. You saw me in a towel. It's only fair."

"Gram could be here any minute."

"Two words," Lily said. "*The Bachelorette.*"

Shane muttered something under his breath but pulled the long-sleeved T-shirt over his head and handed it to her. "Here. Happy?"

The soft fabric was warm from his body and smelled lightly of fresh air with woodsy undertones. She draped it over her shoulder rather than put it on the dusty floor.

"Ecstatic." Then she looked down and the breath left her

body.

The ropy flesh she'd felt under the shirt was in fact lines of tissue marked by scars. Two short, shiny pink lines, one large jagged one and numerous small dots.

He was trembling, his breath fast and shallow.

Valentine got to his feet, padded over and put his head on Shane's leg. Shane stroked him, and his trembling eased.

"What happened?" Lily asked.

"Gunshot wound." Shane's head twitched. "About a year and a half ago. It's mostly healed."

"Did you get mugged?" She sucked in her breath and stepped away as a worse explanation came to her.

"Mugged? No."

"Oh, man. You're not a gang member, are you?"

He gave a short bark of a chuckle. "No. The opposite, actually." He inhaled and then exhaled harshly. "I was a cop."

That's where his military demeanor and concern for her safety came from.

"In Prince George?" she guessed.

He nodded. "I had to come down here for rehab."

"Has it been successful?"

He gave a slight shrug. "Mostly. The overhead painting set it off, though."

"No kidding." She smoothed her palms over the wide expanse of skin. "You're on medical leave, then?"

He made a noncommittal sound. "Yeah."

"When do you have to go back?"

He moved his head to the side and was quiet. "It's not when," he said, after a time. "It's if."

She paused. Go back to police work? Or go back to Prince George? She wanted to ask but sensed he didn't want to talk about it.

Maybe he didn't know.

"Don't stop," he begged.

To have such a strong man admit weakness to her like this was strangely exhilarating—and discomfiting. She could so easily hurt him, without meaning to.

"I'm no masseuse, but does this feel okay?"

He groaned. "Better than okay. I might fall asleep right here."

His obvious pleasure went straight to her head, making her giddy with success. She kneaded and pressed and rubbed, wondering how long he'd been suffering in silence.

"How did it happen?" she asked. "If you don't mind me asking."

He was quiet for a long time. "I was tracking a robbery suspect," he said eventually. "I got cocky, impatient. Stupid. Here I am."

He made it sound like a dumb mistake, a bet he'd lost, the punch line to a bad joke.

"You're lucky you weren't killed."

He stiffened. "Yes. I am."

Valentine whipped his head around, then barked and galloped toward the door.

"Gram's here," Shane said, grabbing his shirt and tugging it back on.

Lily turned to the wall that had the patch of Fog Mist on it and stared at it without seeing. She didn't know if she was about to cry or punch something. She took a deep breath. She needed to get her conflicting mass of emotions under control before Dolly walked in. Especially if she'd brought her friends.

Pretending to be Shane's girlfriend was supposed to be simple. Two people in a temporary bind, helping each other out while standing in solidarity against the unreasonable demands of family.

This felt complicated.

This felt…like it was becoming more.

She brushed her hands against her jeans, but her palms still tingled from the texture of his skin.

Chapter Nine

SHANE HAD OFFERED to take the dog off Lily's hands for the morning, while she ran errands. It would give his shoulder a rest and, he had to admit, Valentine presented an intriguing challenge.

The light rain of earlier had let up so he took the dog into the backyard and tossed the ball. Valentine leaped after it, joy visible in every move he made.

He had an attractive, engaging personality, but the previous neglect had left him so emotionally needy he had a hard time focusing. He was also big, active and he shed profusely. With so many young, undamaged dogs always in need of homes, Valentine wouldn't be anyone's first choice.

"You need a trick," he said to the dog. "A hook. Something to make you stand out. But in a good way."

But he feared it would take nothing short of Valentine being able to fetch a beer from the fridge to get him adopted.

He was just too much dog for most people.

Shane liked big dogs. Well, he liked German shepherds. Titan had weighed almost eighty pounds of pure, beautiful muscle. And that coat was a pain in the ass when it blew out twice a year, leaving clumps of fluffy undercoat everywhere.

And so smart, Shane often thought the dog could read his mind.

Titan had been his constant companion from puppyhood. No wonder they'd been close.

Valentine had been shunted from home to home, person to person, never getting a chance to bond with any one human long enough for someone to uncover his potential.

The dog sat down in front of him, dropped the ball at his feet and whined.

"I think you're smarter than you let on," Shane said.

Val barked.

"Oh yeah?"

Val barked again.

"Really." He put up his hand to keep the dog from barking a third time. Valentine held his peace.

"Good boy."

It shouldn't matter to him whether this animal found a home or not. There were a million homeless dogs in the world and a person could break his heart trying to save them all.

Except for some damn reason this particular dog mattered to Lily. And that mattered to Shane.

He broke off a piece of freeze-dried liver and tossed it to him. Val snatched it out of the air like a frog catching a fly, without breaking his sit.

"You are a smart boy, aren't you?"

What if this was the first time anyone had recognized Val's potential? Most bad behavior in dogs was born of boredom or fear or some unmet need.

All of which described Valentine.

When Shane had been twelve years old, after his third time being sent home from school for fighting, his parents had put him in karate. In the first class, he'd gotten his ass handed to him by a ten-year-old. He threw himself into learning the moves, even the boring katas, burning off all that anger and frustration that came from what was finally discovered to be a mild case of dyslexia. Karate gave him a physical outlet for his energy, and it gave him confidence.

Val didn't tear up Lily's pillows and dig holes in her backyard because he was bad, but because he needed an outlet.

"I need to find your version of karate, buddy." He tossed the ball again and went to the storage shed where Gram had enough stuff to stock a hardware store.

Within thirty minutes, using a few lengths of PVC pipe, some leftover two-by-fours and spare bits of plywood, he had a makeshift agility course.

Well, two jumps and a stay table.

He attached Val's leash and walked him toward the first jump. It was about six inches off the ground, hardly a barrier for a dog his size.

Val walked up to it, then stopped and looked at Shane.

"Jump over it, bud," Shane said.

But the dog walked around the other side.

Shane kept leading him but picked up the pace, approaching the second jump at an easy jog. This time, he tightened the leash so that there was nowhere else for Valentine to go and no time to stop.

Val hopped over it without even slowing down.

"Good boy!" Shane bent down and ruffled the dog's ears. Val leaped up against him, knocking the jump over with his tail. It didn't matter. He'd done the right thing.

Then Shane put the two jumps in a row, a few paces apart. Holding the leash away from his body, he led Val toward them again at a slow run. Val jumped the first and then the second, then turned and looked at Shane as if to say, "Well, where's my treat, man?"

"You are a very, very good boy!" Shane praised him and rewarded him with treats.

The dog's heeling skills were improving, but only on leash. Would Val jump on command, off leash?

He unclipped the leash and started to run around the yard again, slowly. As he expected, Val joined him. It was a simple matter to direct the dog toward the jumps and this time, Val took them with deliberate strides. He'd figured it out.

"Oh, man." Shane thumped the dog on his rib cage and gave him more treats. "You're brilliant, Valentine!"

He'd forgotten how much fun running the obstacle course was. Titan had practiced it as part of his police dog training, so that he would be prepared to work under as wide a range of circumstances as might present themselves in his daily work.

He ran around the yard a few more times. He couldn't

wait to show Lily what they'd learned today. She'd be so thrilled. He could imagine her competing with Val, her hair trailing behind her as she ran, her cheeks flushed with excitement and success.

The same way her cheeks turned pink when she was flustered. Like when she'd stood in front of him in nothing but a towel.

Or how she might look if he kissed her.

He could imagine her soft hair trailing through his fingers as he cupped the side of her face, the sweetness of her lips against his, the look of dark promise in her eyes.

He shook off his train of thought and glanced at his watch. Lily would be finished with her errands soon. He should bring Val back. Gram's wishful thinking had no business putting ideas into his head that did not belong there.

"Come on, boy. Let's go get you cleaned up."

He brushed out the dog's coat on the patio. It was growing back nicely. Soon, the scars would be invisible.

Poor bastard. How long had he suffered with those wounds? And how was it that his disposition was still so pure, so sweet?

If only people could be so resilient.

If only he could be so resilient.

Maybe then, he'd have a chance at a real relationship again. Maybe even with someone as great as Lily. She deserved someone a hell of a lot better than him.

"Good job, buddy." The dog leaped off the porch and

shook, flapping his long ears and wiggling all over with pleasure.

He hoped that whatever family Val went to would be willing to do agility with him. The dog was a natural.

Tomorrow, he'd build some more jumps and maybe a weave pole. He could bring out the sawhorses, for an elevated walkway and maybe even make a teeter-totter.

It wasn't fetching a beer from the fridge, but agility would certainly set Valentine apart.

Would it be enough?

THE NEXT DAY, Lily was two hours into organizing a spreadsheet of annual foundation events when her cell phone buzzed.

Ariel.

She answered the call, happy to take a break. Any day now, the caterer would be demanding final numbers for the next Kovac Foundation benefit dinner and Marisa was dithering on the guest list.

"Hey Ariel," she said. "Which would you rather pay $1000 for: scallops or prawns?"

"I do not understand your world," the shelter manager said.

"Not my world," Lily corrected. "My mother's world. You're probably calling to check up on Valentine, aren't you?"

"How's he doing?"

She closed her laptop and set it aside, moving from her cozy home office, where Valentine lay snoozing in his crate, to the living room.

It was ridiculous, but she didn't want to talk about the dog while he could overhear her.

"So far today, he's only destroyed one pair of socks. That's a big improvement from yesterday, when he stole a loaf of bread off the counter, dug a gigantic hole in my yard and terrorized the paper delivery girl through the window."

Ariel was quiet. "Are you giving him lots of exercise?"

"An hour in the park, twice a day," Lily said. "Ariel, I hope I haven't taken on more than I can handle. I thought I could do this, but some days, I think he's actually getting worse." She hesitated, not wanting to sound petty. "He doesn't seem very interested in me. He's got a big crush on this random stranger we met at the park, though."

She told herself it didn't matter that Valentine had switched alliances. He was a foster dog. It was better for them both if they weren't bonded.

But did he have to show such a blatant preference for Shane?

The rejection stung. It wasn't rejection, actually. It was disinterest and that was far, far worse.

Ariel laughed. "I take it this stranger is male. Is he hot? Interesting? Available?"

"He's an ex-cop from Prince George who makes me feel like an idiot who can't handle a dog."

"You're not an idiot. And it doesn't sound like he's a complete stranger anymore. How much time have you spent together?"

"I pass by his house every day on the way to the park," she admitted. "Turns out, he needed some decorating advice, so he's helping me with the dog, in exchange. He's a decent teacher. I'm learning a lot. I wish I could say the same for Valentine. Shane says I'm not firm enough but after everything this poor dog's been through, I can't bring myself to be harsh."

But that wasn't being fair. Shane was never harsh. She thought about how quiet he'd gotten when they'd discovered Valentine's scars, how gentle and careful he'd been with the clippers to keep from hurting the dog more.

"Sounds like they've connected," Ariel said. "Do you think he might want to adopt Valentine?"

"I've had the same thought, but he says absolutely not." She realized that Shane had never said exactly why he didn't want Valentine. "He had dogs growing up, he said, but doesn't have one now. Or maybe he has one waiting for him back at home. He came down here after being injured on the job."

She forced herself to slow down. If she kept going on and on about the man, Ariel would sense that there was more to their relationship than neighbors trading services.

"Wait a second," Ariel said. "A cop. From Prince George. What's his last name?"

"Bowman. Why?"

"Hang on. I know this. Gimme a sec. It's in here somewhere."

Lily imagined her friend holding up a finger, her eyes closed in concentration as she rifled through her prodigious memory for the random bits of animal-related news and knowledge that settled there, waiting to become useful.

She told herself the curiosity she felt was only normal. But anticipation built with each second.

Then she heard a huge intake of air and Ariel was squealing. The tap-tap-tapping sound told her that Ariel had leaped online for confirmation.

"Oh my God, oh my God, oh my God! Do you have any idea who you've been dealing with?"

Lily held her cell phone away from her ear. "I think you're about to tell me."

"I am," Ariel confirmed, with a breathless hush. "You, my dear, oblivious pal, have had the privilege of working with a genuine hero."

"You mean when he got shot in the shoulder? It sounded pretty bad."

Lily walked to her front bay window, which faced the direction of the park, swallowing disappointment. This wasn't news. One street over, just beyond those trees, Shane was no doubt working through pain to get back on schedule. His commitment was bordering on foolhardy. But she couldn't deny his love for Dolly.

"Pretty bad?" Ariel echoed, sounding like she was about to faint. "He almost died. Did he tell you that?"

"What? No."

"Yes. It gets better. He ran through the woods for over a mile, carrying his partner, who'd been stabbed and shot, too. Did he tell you that?"

"No." Lily felt behind her for a kitchen chair and lowered herself onto it.

"Did Sergeant Bowman tell you while he was running, he radioed the location of the suspect's next target, a gentleman in his eighties? The suspect was arrested on the victim's doorstep. Sergeant Bowman's information saved that man's life."

Now Lily felt faint. "No. He didn't mention any of this."

"Did he mention," Ariel continued, her voice thick with emotion, "that his partner bled to death in his arms?"

Oh, Shane. He put on such a stoic face.

"How...how do you know all this?" she asked her friend.

But before the words were fully out, Lily knew the heartbreaking answer.

There was only one reason an animal shelter manager would be so taken by the heroism of a cop from a small northern town.

It explained why Shane was so good with Valentine—and why he couldn't return the dog's affection.

"His partner." Tears prickled at the back of Lily's eyes. "Shane's partner was a dog, wasn't he?"

Chapter Ten

Lily opened Valentine's crate. "Come on, boy. Let's go for a car ride."

She needed to get out of the house. She had to do something, had to go somewhere she could be outside and breathe and think, without the possibility of running into Shane.

Her usual route through the park wouldn't do.

Ariel's revelation had shaken her to her core. It would take time to process the information before she dared see him again.

Valentine jumped gracefully into the back of her car, always eager for new sights. He'd filled out in the weeks he'd been with her and gotten stronger, too. His ribs were barely visible. The once dull and matted fur was now soft and shiny and thick enough that the scars were no longer visible. He was even learning to tolerate the collar, though she still used the harness most of the time.

She drove across the bridge to the north side of the river, with no conscious destination in mind, only knowing that she needed someplace peaceful, with trees and grass and quiet, where she could shed a few tears, if necessary.

When she reached the rolling riverlands on the edge of

town, she almost laughed through the lump in her throat. Of course she'd end up here.

She clipped the leash to Valentine's harness and he jumped down, calmer than usual, as if recognizing her emotional turmoil.

She hadn't been here in ages. But it felt exactly right.

They followed the footpath that wended through the low-growing shrubs and grasses and blackberry vines nestled against the broad bank of the river.

"Hey, Daddy," she whispered.

This place, where her father had often come to walk when he was troubled, was also now his final resting place. His ashes nourished the ferns and rushes next to the rippling water just as his spirit whispered to her through the bare branches, easing her soul.

Quiet, long-suffering Frank Garner had also been a hero, if not to the world, then to the daughter who was so much like him.

She let Valentine explore the mossy bank, sniffing and digging to his heart's content.

"I think I'm in trouble, Daddy." She tossed a pebble into the river. "I found somebody. And he's a good guy. A really good guy. But he's sort of...broken."

She looked at Valentine. He was broken, too, a rehabilitation project every bit as complex as Dolly's house. Or Shane's shoulder, for that matter.

With the right family, he'd make a good pet. She smiled sadly. They still had work to do. But she trusted that Ariel would find the right people who would love Valentine the way he needed to be loved.

Broken didn't have to be permanent.

Shane had despised her pity over his injured shoulder. She wouldn't be able to hide her heartbreak over the depth of his loss and intuitively she knew he would hate that.

Ariel, with her single-minded dedication to the animal shelter, wanted to include Shane in the February Adoption Option event. Since the flood, the need for funds was even more desperate. Having a decorated police dog handler train one of their rescue dogs would bring great public attention to their work, maybe coverage from the local cable network.

They always tied the event in with Valentine's Day. Imagine how much attention a dog called Valentine would get.

The thought should have made her happy. She wanted him to find a good home. That was the whole point of caring for him all this time.

But would people want Valentine for the right reasons? Would they see him for the fun, sweet animal he was? Or would they want to be able to say they had the dog with the sad story they'd seen on TV? Who'd been trained by a genuine hero?

Shane would never agree.

Ariel urged her not to tell him about her scheme until she'd ironed out all the details. She was certain that once they had a solid plan, and Lily warmed Shane up to the idea, he'd be happy to lend his fame to the cause.

Lily wished she had Ariel's confidence.

She had a feeling that when Shane learned about this, he'd wish he'd never met Valentine.

Or her.

AFTER A WEEK of colder weather that included a skiff of snow one night, a day of sunshine was most welcome. Lily was in the park with Shane and Valentine again and, as usual, the dog was listening moderately well to Shane. To Lily, he was listening not at all, distracted by every child, bike, bird and squirrel in a ten-kilometer radius. She couldn't wait until spring arrived, imagining Valentine racing among the plum and cherry trees dripping with blossoms.

Except Valentine would be long gone by then.

Shane too, probably.

She shook the thoughts from her head. She needed to bring the conversation around to the Adoption Option event, and Ariel's hope that he'd be part of the festivities.

The board of directors—fortunately or unfortunately, depending on your point of view—had been ecstatic about having Shane participate.

The simple open house, as the event had been in the past, had been scrapped in favor of something much larger, in a different venue, all details yet to be determined.

The bleat of her cell phone sounded from inside her jacket pocket. Lily pulled it out.

"It's my mom," she said.

Shane put his hands on his hips. "Are we doing this or not? If you're not paying attention, why should he?"

He was attempting to teach her how to keep Valentine focused on her, rather than lunging at walkers and joggers, an ongoing problem for the excitable dog.

"I know, I know." Lily let the call go to voice mail, switched off the sound and put the phone back in her pocket. Marisa would be mad, but it wouldn't be the first time.

"Okay, I'm listening. Now what?"

He never mentioned Titan, and the information Ariel had shared with her weighed heavily on her conscience.

It wasn't like it was a secret.

But if he wanted her to know, he'd have told her himself.

Nor did he talk about what he'd be doing once the house was finished. Or his life in Prince George. Or police work.

With so much they couldn't talk about, conversation was rather stilted at times.

They were friends who were training a dog together and occasionally held hands when Dolly was watching.

Her pocket vibrated again.

Shane raised his eyebrows. "I thought you turned it off."

Lily groaned. Marisa, again. "I better take this. She gets...well. She won't give up until I answer."

Shane huffed and took Valentine's leash from her. "I'll practice heeling with him until you're ready to work."

"Mom, hi," Lily said, making a face at him. "I'm in the middle of something. Can I call you back?"

"Surely you can spare a few minutes." Marisa sounded hurt and immediately Lily felt bad.

"Sorry. How are you?"

Belatedly, she realized that since she'd blown off the so-called family dinner Marisa had wanted her to attend last Saturday, Lily owed her mother some cooperation. At least, that's how Marisa would see it.

"Concerned. You've been spending so much time with that dog, I'm worried you're neglecting the foundation. Is everything ready for the junior symphony fund-raiser this weekend?"

Lily sighed. "Every ducky is quacking in a row."

"Have you spoken with the caterer? The conductor is deathly allergic to shellfish and her husband is gluten free and oh, they're both vegans."

"I've banned shellfish and I always order vegan and gluten-free options. You know this, Mother."

"And your companion for the evening, dear? I've taken the liberty—"

"Mom," Lily warned. "Don't."

"But—"

"No." Lily turned her back, hoping Shane couldn't overhear. "Remember? I'm seeing someone. Shane. You met him."

"The dog trainer?" The pleading disappeared from Marisa's tone and in its place came the iron hammer of implacability. "Have fun with him if you must but he's hardly a suitable escort for the symphony."

Lily closed her eyes and willed herself to stay calm. How much longer could she stand this? Maybe she could beg Sara to return early? Say, in exchange for a lifetime of babysitting?

Shane led the dog around in front of her and pointed to his watch.

"Mom, I've got to go. See you on Saturday."

But Marisa went on as if Lily hadn't spoken. "Ilona McGovern's eldest son, Radisson, just broke up with his longtime girlfriend and will be joining us for the evening. I've asked Ilona to arrive early so I can introduce the two of you before the activities commence. I'm sure you'll get along famously."

"Mom. Did you even hear me?"

"You will be accompanied by an appropriate bachelor," Marisa said. "It's either Radisson or Chad. You decide."

"Mom!"

"Oh, fine. Bring your friend Shane, if you like," Marisa said, giving in too easily. "Do you think he has a tuxedo?"

Damn. She'd called Lily's bluff.

"God, Mother, you're impossible."

"Radisson, then. Good."

"No!"

If Marisa wanted her with a man, she'd bring one of her own choosing. Maybe this would teach her mother to quit meddling.

She pressed the phone to her ear and squeezed her eyes shut. "Shane and I will see you on Saturday."

"Black tie," Marisa said.

"I know." She shot a quick glance at Shane, who'd taken a step closer. He was listening avidly now.

Heat crept into her cheeks.

A smile played around the corners of Shane's lips. He was enjoying it, the bastard. She met his gaze and held it.

"Lily?" Marisa said.

"It'll be fine, Mom. I've gotta go." She clicked the end button, turned off the ringer and pocketed her phone.

Shane's eyebrows shot up. "I take it I've got a role to play?"

"Any chance," she asked, hoping she didn't look as desperate as she felt, "you like orchestral music?"

"I'M MORE OF a country-rock fan myself."

Shane found Lily's discomfort highly amusing. Her face was flaming, but she held her head up high.

"How much did you hear?" she demanded.

"Enough to know that you're about to invite me on a very fancy date."

"It's a fund-raiser for the junior symphony." She grimaced.

"Surely they're not that bad."

"They're wonderful and I'm happy that we're supporting them. That's not it." She shoved her fists deep into the pockets of her sweatshirt, hunching her shoulders. "She caught me off guard and...I blanked. You don't have to come. I'll tell her you got sick at the last minute or something."

He walked in a wide circle, pleased to see Valentine staying more or less at heel. The dog had accepted a soft martingale collar for training though Lily still preferred the harness for ordinary exercise walks.

"Are you going?"

"I have to."

"Is there a gun to your head?"

That earned him a ghost of a smile. "It's sort of my job."

"I thought you were an interior designer."

"By day. By night, I'm a reluctant event planner, hostess with the mostess. My mother likes to think of the Kovac Foundation as a family business."

He stopped. "The Kovac Foundation." Where had he heard of that before? Then it came to him, something in the newspaper about a society function. "That's you?"

Valentine whined.

"My mother, not me," she corrected. "But yeah, that's the one."

He snapped his fingers and started another circle, in the opposite direction, but his mind wasn't on the dog.

Lily Garner was an honest to God heiress.

No wonder Marisa Rollins's response to seeing him with her daughter had been chilly. She was wealthy, connected and traveled in circles that didn't include scruffy small-town ex-lawmen.

He'd never have guessed that Lily came from such a

background. She seemed so down-to-earth.

Step, step, step. Walk, walk, walk. The dog kept pace, but his tail was at half-mast. He was very sensitive to the emotions around him. Shane relaxed his grip on the leash.

"You're what, her event planner?"

Lily nodded glumly. "Personal assistant, general manager, overall peon."

"Interior design is just a hobby?"

"If my mother had her way." She let her cheeks puff out as she exhaled. "The foundation is her life and she doesn't understand why I'm not interested in running it with her. Sara, my sister, loves it and she's very good at it, much better than I am. She and Mom are very similar but since the birth of the only begotten grandchild, Mom's stuck with me. I think she's hoping I'll come to my senses and give up my own career."

She put air quotes around the word career, as if it was a joke she'd long since decided to accept, even though she didn't find it funny.

It wasn't right.

It also wasn't his business.

A dead leaf fluttered across the path in front of them and Valentine darted after it, nearly tripping Shane.

He deserved that.

He untangled the leash and redirected the dog. "What does your dad think?"

Lily looked away. Her gaze turned inward, as if she was looking at something long ago and far away. "He passed away years ago. Construction accident. Hard to believe my high-maintenance mother was once a contractor's wife." She swallowed. "Mom doesn't like to talk about those days."

This bright-eyed daughter, with leaf litter in her hair and dirt under her nails, who had a tool set and sawhorses in her garage, was a living reminder of that time.

Lily shivered, as if to shrug off the memories, like Valentine shaking off bathwater. "I don't mind organizing the events, but I hate that I'm required to attend them as well. Accompanied by a man, of course, so it appears that I'm there as a guest and not, as she puts it, the help."

"A man of her choosing," he guessed.

"Happily single is not a concept she's familiar with."

"Your mom and my grandmother have a lot in common."

Lily burst out laughing. "I sincerely doubt that. But they do share this one sentiment. Listen, Shane, I didn't mean to drag you into this. We weren't serious about the whole pretend-dating thing. I can handle another evening of inane conversation with some stuffy hedge fund manager. I've done it before, I can do it again."

Heiress or not, the idea of Lily spending her evening with some smug, entitled, penguin-suited muckety-muck didn't sit well. She deserved to be with someone who appreciated her sharp wit and kind nature, not just her pedigree.

But he had no business presuming to know what was best for her.

"Maybe this hedge fund manager will be nice," he said.

"I'm the daughter of Marisa Kovac Garner Rollins," Lily said in a plummy voice. Then she thinned her lips. "He'll be whatever he has to be."

That sat even worse with him. No wonder Lily was skeptical about her mother's setups. He tried to picture her in the glamorous world she described. But all he saw was a woman with her hair caught up in a ponytail, her cheeks pink from fresh air, with yellow dog hair on her black jogging pants.

Valentine yelped and jumped up against him.

"Off," he commanded and set off walking in yet another circle, wishing his thoughts were so easy to manage.

"I'll go with you if you want," he said, not quite knowing where the offer had come from.

He'd spent the past however many months avoiding people as much as possible. He had no use for small talk and hated the prospect of answering questions about himself.

It was a horrible idea. Two people couldn't be less suited. Even though he usually saw her in jogging outfits, Lily probably had a closet full of couture gowns. Shane had jeans and flannel shirts.

Nevertheless, he was comfortable with her. He liked that she didn't know anything about him, or his history. She didn't feel sorry for him, or call him a hero, or tell him how great he was for the sacrifices he'd made.

Even working with Valentine, which he did not want to do, didn't think he could do, was okay. Fun, even. No one expected much from a rescue dog. Low expectations meant little risk of failure, exactly what Shane needed right now.

"It's not your responsibility to rescue me from my mother's paternalistic, patriarchal paradigm," Lily said. "But thank you, anyway."

"Wow," he said. "Those are a lot of big words."

"I've been practicing them for years."

Shane handed the leash to Lily and directed her to walk with Valentine herself, correcting when necessary and praising as much as possible.

"I'd never presume to rescue you from anything, Lily," he said, once she and Valentine were in sync. "You're obviously someone who can take care of herself."

"Oh yeah?" She reached down and gave Valentine a pat.

"I mean it. But if you want me to go with you, I will."

Lily didn't enjoy working for the foundation, yet she did it for her mother. He wouldn't enjoy this, but he would do it, for Lily.

She looked up, startled. "Really?"

"Sure. Unless you're trying to bargain your way out of time with Gram and her gal pals," he said.

Her laughter pealed. "I wouldn't dream of it."

"Good. Do I really have to wear a tux?"

She gave him a quick once-over. "Wear something nice."

He thought of his red serge dress uniform, carefully packed in dry-cleaners' plastic, wondered what she'd think, if she saw him in it.

Didn't matter. He'd never wear it again.

"How nice?" he asked.

She pursed her lips, thinking. "Nice enough not to get kicked out. Not so nice that my mother wants you for a son-in-law."

That made him laugh. "I can work with that."

Chapter Eleven

On the night of the symphony fund-raiser, Lily was waiting for him on the steps in front of the wide, curved driveway. He got out, handing his keys to the waiting valet, hoping he wasn't too underdressed.

He'd bought a new suit for the occasion and Gram had assured him he looked fine.

But Lily looked a hell of a lot better than fine.

"Hello!" She leaned in, rested her hand briefly on his chest and brushed a kiss against his cheek. Light as a butterfly, fragrant as a flower, fleeting as a falling star, here then gone. Sweet, polite and utterly unsatisfying, it had the unsettling effect of rendering him speechless.

"Shane?"

If the touch of her lips on his skin hadn't stolen his breath, the image that met his eyes when she's stepped back, would have.

She wore a shimmery dress that shone different colors as she moved and clung to curves he hadn't known she had. Her eyes were heavily made up, her lashes long and dense, her lush lips shiny. Her hair was pinned up in a complicated arrangement that left only a few blonde locks curling at her throat. He wanted to take out the pins and free the rest of that golden mass so she'd look at least a little like the Lily he knew.

He willed himself to speak.

"You look..." He blew out a breath, not sure how to finish the sentence. "Like something from a magazine."

She raised her eyebrows. "I hope that's a good thing. You clean up nice too. Come on. I'll show you where to stand for the best view."

The people watching, she'd told him, would be excellent.

She led him into the foyer, where Marisa was exchanging air kisses with an older couple. He stood next to Lily while she greeted guests with her mother, who introduced him by name only, with no further explanation, as if referring to him even as Lily's friend would be too much recognition.

The trickle of arrivals turned to a flood, people turning out in force to support the junior symphony. The crowd was polite, but they all seemed to know each other and have little interest in those who didn't fit their specific mold.

He didn't care. He wasn't there for them.

"Marisa, darling, who is this treasure?"

The man approaching Marisa distinguished himself among the sea of black-clad bodies with a bright blue bow tie. His eyes were trained on Lily, completely ignoring Shane, which was just fine. He preferred to observe, anyway. The body language of these people fascinated him. So much touching, so many outbursts of pleasure and interest that were, in fact, revelations of subordination bordering on desperation.

Beta pups begging for scraps.

Marisa smiled and slipped her hand into the crook of Lily's arm, no doubt to keep her from running away. Shane wished she would but knew she wouldn't. She didn't shirk her obligations.

Marisa greeted the man by name, then tipped her head slightly and gave Lily a smile that made Shane's teeth ache. "This is my daughter."

"Ah." The treasure hunter took her hand and gave it a half-lift, half-shake, as if he'd intended to kiss it but changed his mind at the last second. "The lovely and talented Sara. I've heard so much about you."

Lily's smile tightened. A pained expression flitted across her eyes.

"Oh!" Marisa laughed. "This isn't Sara. This is my other daughter, Lily." She paused to take a breath, blinked and continued, her voice a bright tinkle. "Darling, you remember Elijah Highsmith."

Marisa turned then to Shane, her movement as tight and squeaky as the Tin Man's on the Yellow Brick Road.

"Elijah, this is...um, my daughter's..." Whether her pause was because she couldn't remember his name, or didn't know how to categorize him, he wasn't sure. He was beginning to understand some of Lily's angst.

"Dog trainer," Shane said, reaching for Elijah's hand. "Shane Bowman. Pleased to meet you."

"Dog trainer." Elijah's eyebrows rose. He shot Marisa an

amused look that told Shane there would be much conversation about this later.

"Mr. Highsmith is a writer and very involved in the art world," Marisa said. "We're always so happy to have him here."

Highsmith nodded. "Thank you for having me." He turned to Lily. "Delighted to make your acquaintance, miss. Tell me, are you also artistic?"

Lily's smile had a desperate intensity to it. Hectic color flooded her cheeks. She started to speak but Marisa took charge of the conversation, swatting the writer's arm gently.

"Oh, Eli. Not everyone can be an artist, you know. Besides, Lily's much too busy working for the foundation."

"Actually," Lily broke in, "I have a degree in design and hope to open my own firm one day."

Shane looked at her in surprise. Good for her.

"How nice." But Highsmith's eyes had already glazed over.

Marisa leaped in, determined to steer the conversation elsewhere. "Sweetheart, fetch Eli a fresh glass of champagne. We can't let our guests go thirsty, can we?"

A woman with long red hair and a flame-colored gown walked past them and the art critic's eyes came back to life.

"Actually, if you'll excuse me," he said, bowing slightly. "It was a pleasure to meet you, Millie."

The flush in Lily's cheeks deepened. A muscle in her jaw twitched. "Enjoy the party," she said tightly.

Another sparkly person captured Marisa's attention and

as soon as she was gone, Shane drew closer to Lily. "Tell me more about yourself, Millie," he whispered.

She threw him a dark glare. "Don't start with me. I'm in a killing mood."

She was quivering, her fingers knotted together, her expression brittle. But beneath the angry ice lay a river of bone-deep hurt. She was a property without trade value to her mother, invisible in this crowd, and she knew it.

"Lily," he said softly.

"Don't." The word shook. Her lips barely moved. "Don't say anything nice. There's ten pounds of makeup on my face and one nice word from you will ruin it. So be mean. Be rude. Be yourself. That's the only way I'll get through this."

He wanted to wring Highsmith's scrawny throat. He wanted to shake Marisa. He wanted to stand up on the bar and let the room know that Lily Garner was here, and how were they not celebrating that?

How where they not cherishing her?

But he swallowed his indignation and gave her what she asked for.

"You're crabby. You need some food." He lifted a platter from a startled waiter, ignored his protest and pushed Lily quickly through the crowd.

He found a small table in a quiet corner and pushed her onto the stool. "Sit. Stay."

"Where are you going?" she asked, her eyes wide.

"To get you a beer."

He didn't care if the bar was stocked only with party-themed cocktails and champagne, Lily Garner was getting a Guinness.

BY THE TIME Shane made his way back through the crowd, two frothy glasses in his hands, Lily had regained her composure. She didn't care about Elijah Highsmith. But the fact that he didn't remember her at all, he who appeared at every one of her mother's events, and had seen Lily at least a dozen times, was utterly humiliating.

Shane had a good five inches on the man, and she hadn't missed the way Elijah had puffed out his chest when they stood side by side. As if that would help.

He was the only man in the room not wearing a tux, yet when he stood next to her, instead of appearing underdressed, he made everyone else look overdressed. He was proud, unapologetic and utterly at ease.

"You look like Moses, parting the Red Sea." She accepted the glass. "I can't believe they had it. I set the bar menu myself. This was not on it."

"The bartender was happy to accommodate a special request from the host."

"You said my mother wanted beer?" Marisa would have a fit.

"A fake boyfriend's gotta do what a fake boyfriend's gotta do." He slid into the seat next to hers and touched the rim of his glass to hers. "Sláinte."

"To surviving tonight with our senses of humor intact." She took a sip, then drank deeply. The dark Irish stout slipped down her throat, instantly making her feel better, more like herself. She had nothing against champagne. But it was associated with the demands of social events she'd prefer to avoid.

She was so very tired of being judged and found wanting. There was something freeing about this small act of defiance.

Shane nudged another platter of canapés her way. "Eat."

She looked at the variety of finger foods and her stomach gave a low rumble. As usual, she'd skipped lunch in the crush of preparations. She was used to suppressing her appetite, Marisa having impressed upon her many times the importance of self-restraint.

"'Men aren't attracted to gluttons,'" she said, making air quotes with her fingers.

"You fill out your dress a hell of a lot better than Highsmith's redhead does." Shane gave a half-shrug. "Not that it matters to you because you're not trying to attract a man."

"That's right. I'm not." She looked at the platter but saw nothing, so sharp was her surprise at the compliment. Instead of Sara and Marisa's small-boned elegance, she had her father's athletic build. A size zero she was not.

Her appetite returned with a rush. To heck with Marisa's rules. "Spanakopita, my favorite."

She lifted a tiny piece of spinach and cheese-filled pastry and popped it in her mouth. The tender flaky crust had just the right amount of texture and the tart, creamy inside made her moan in pleasure.

"Oh, my God. I'd forgotten how good these were." While she was still chewing, she put two more onto a cloth napkin.

"You really like spinach." Shane's voice was hoarse.

"I like the Greek version," she said. "It's good for you. Full of iron. Have some."

He chuckled. "Thanks, but you look like a wolf standing over a fresh kill."

"Ha, ha." The prosciutto-wrapped dates were also delicious. As were the bruschetta bites.

"Feeling better?"

Shane looked at her over the rim of his glass. She didn't know what to make of the concern that lurked in the back of his eyes.

"I don't need your sympathy," she said. "I've been embarrassed before; I'll be embarrassed again. No big deal."

He pursed his lips, then looked away, without speaking.

"What?" she said.

"Nothing," he replied. "It's your party. I'm just a guest, here at your request."

"It's not my party. It's my mother's party."

She knew what it looked like. But he didn't understand how important it was to Marisa to present a united front. Lily couldn't bear to disappoint her mother. Yes, there was a personal cost sometimes, but what was she supposed to do? Let Marisa hire some stranger who wouldn't understand her?

"This is a temporary situation." She didn't owe him an explanation, but she didn't want him to think of her as a victim. "Once my sister comes back, Mother won't need me. Sara's a social butterfly and much better at all this than I am anyway."

Again, he watched her without speaking. She had to fight the urge to fill the silence. Is that what he wanted? To keep her talking? Well. Two could play at that game.

She turned her attention to the olive tapenade.

"Don't look now," he said, nodding toward the redhead in the scarlet dress. "Carrot-Top is about to give Elijah High-and-Mighty the heave-ho."

The most spectacular woman in the room and he referred to her as Carrot-Top? "She's a very successful model. Every man in this room would like to be in Elijah's shoes."

"Not every man." Shane shifted position, leaning closer to speak directly into her ear. "See how she's got her arms crossed? She's about to tell old Eli to take a hike."

His breath tickled her neck, sending frissons of electricity down her body and making her shiver. "I doubt it. He's Elijah Highsmith, you know."

"She's not impressed."

She looked at the couple again. Perhaps Elijah's interest wasn't returned. "How do you know that?"

"Well, first of all, she appears to have a functional brain."

She bit back a laugh. "Yeah, that's what most men would notice about her."

"I'm not most men, if you haven't picked up on that

yet."

She turned and met his eyes, thinking about what Ariel had told her about him, wondering how, when or even whether to broach the subject of Titan's award. "There's definitely more to you than meets the eye."

He leaned forward again, and she caught a whiff of his cologne, something subtle, woodsy. "Look at her feet."

Lily glanced at the model's heels. "Manolo Blahniks. What about them?"

"See where they're pointing? The door. It's a dead giveaway. First chance she gets, she's taking off."

"No way. She wouldn't risk offending him. You might know body language, but I know this crowd."

He smiled. "What do you bet?"

"Nothing. You're wrong, I'm right. Any second, she's going to lean in, show a little more boobage, and take his arm."

"So, you're sure, then?"

"This ain't my first rodeo, Irish."

He grinned at that. "Then you won't be afraid to wager, Greek. Look closer. See how Redhead is pinching the skin between her thumb and forefinger? She's taken a step back, too. She wouldn't touch Elijah with a ten-foot pole."

It was difficult to focus with Shane so close to her. She could feel the heat of his body coming from where he'd loosened his tie and opened the top button of his dress shirt.

How she envied his ability to be himself. It didn't matter to him that he didn't fit in, that people were looking at him, wondering what he was doing here, probably laughing behind their manicured hands. She wished it didn't matter to her.

"You underestimate them both."

"I bet you a kiss you're wrong."

Lily turned. "Excuse me?"

"Simple. I say Red's going to walk away. You say she won't. If I'm right, you owe me a kiss."

"You're delirious."

"Okay, be a chicken."

She crossed her arms and faced him. "And what if I'm right?"

"Then I owe you a kiss?"

"Dreamer." But something deep inside her awakened. She hadn't been kissed in a very long time. Hadn't wanted to be kissed in even longer.

Not that she wanted this hypothetical kiss at all. From him. Right now.

"If I'm right and you're wrong," she said, thinking quickly, "you give my mother some excuse, make it a good one, and get us out of here."

She wasn't the least bit surprised when the beautiful redhead put her hand on Elijah's arm and walked with him to a quieter corner of the room.

What did surprise her was her disappointment at seeing Shane lose. He'd been so certain that he'd get that kiss from her.

"See?" she said. "I'm sure she loathes him as much as you

say she does. But he's useful to her. That's how you get ahead, Shane. It's called networking."

"That's one word for it." He sighed. "Okay, you win."

He pulled out his phone and began texting.

"What are you doing?"

He finished the message and hit the send button. "A big interior design job, coming your way. Just what your new firm needs."

A buzz sounded from inside her bag. "Shane, I was only goading my mother. I'm not seriously opening my own business."

"Why not?"

She had a million reasons, starting with the foundation, continuing with her teaching job and ending with fear of failure.

He held up his phone, as her purse continued to buzz. "You have to take this right now. No choice. Your career's on the line. Your mom will understand."

He looked at her like she was the only woman in the room. It made her feel beautiful and powerful and special. "I was just kidding, Shane. You can go, but I should stay. Thanks for coming with me, I appreciate it."

"Nope," he said. "A bet's a bet. I'd have definitely demanded that kiss. Get your coat. We're splitting this pop stand."

IT WASN'T OFTEN that the Dairy Queen saw patrons in semi-formal dress. Probably only high-school grads on prom night. But Lily couldn't have cared less. Anywhere was better than the brittle room full of people her mother deemed important.

"Extra-large hot fudge sundae with peanuts and marsh-mallow cream," she said, when the counter person looked up at her. "What? I'm hungry."

The kid said nothing, just keyed in her order.

"Excellent choice, madam," murmured Shane from behind her. "The cacao was superb that year."

"And you?" said the kid, looking at Shane.

"I'm good." He pulled out his wallet.

"Wait!" Lily looked at him. "I just ordered this huge, decadent sundae. You're not going to let me eat alone, are you?"

He smiled and handed the server a twenty-dollar bill. "That thing is going to be bigger than your head. You'll never finish it yourself."

"Says who? I'm always starving after a fund-raiser dinner. It takes a lot of energy to be polite when what I really want to do is start a food fight."

The counter boy looked up in alarm.

"Don't worry," she told him. "I'm over it."

Shane carried the tray with the giant, dripping dessert to a melamine two-top and pushed it toward her. "For what it's worth, I think a little screaming and food throwing might be cathartic."

"I'm fine. My shelter work neutralizes the toxins nicely. We'll have a lot more fun at the adoption event, I promise."

He raised his eyebrows. "We?"

"You want to be there to make sure Valentine is on his best behavior, don't you? So he can find his forever family?"

A cloud flitted across his face. "Sure. I guess."

Lily kept her attention on the ice cream but his response triggered a rush of hope inside her. He didn't like the idea of Valentine being adopted. He was getting attached! Enough to adopt Valentine himself? It was the perfect solution, only Shane hadn't realized it yet. Pushing him wouldn't work. She just had to pretend she didn't care and make sure that he and the dog spent as much time together as possible.

Then she had to trust that Shane would come to his senses before it was too late.

She took a red plastic spoon—he'd gotten two, the know-it-all—and dug in.

She moaned. "Oh, man. This is exactly what I needed." She let the sweet cold mouthful melt on her tongue, savoring the salty counterpoint crunch of the peanuts.

Shane was watching her with a strange expression on his face.

"What?" she said, taking another big bite.

"Nothing." He blinked and gave his head a little shake. "When's the last time you had one of these?"

She thought. "I don't know. Probably not since I was a kid."

"Really? But it's one of your favorite spots, you said."

She nodded, shrugging. "Guilty pleasure. You caught me in a weak moment."

"Oh, Millie."

She pointed a spoonful of ice cream at him. "Do not start with me, Shane. I am not in the mood."

In fact, her mood had improved considerably since leaving her mother's gala. The image of Marisa standing there in disbelief as Shane said their goodbyes would go a long way to pushing out the memory of Elijah Highsmith's dismissal.

"Give me a taste," Shane said. He leaned forward and opened his mouth.

He had good teeth, straight and clean and strong. As she placed the spoon onto his tongue, she felt the resistance, the cheap plastic not enough to keep her from imagining the soft slide that tongue might make against her own mouth.

"Mm," he said, catching a drip of chocolate with his fingertip. "Good. You should do this more often."

"Get all dressed up to hang out in a fast-food joint? Or feed you my ice cream?"

They'd barely made a dent on the sundae. He was right. She'd never be able to finish it on her own.

He gazed at her, then blinked, his long, dark eyelashes sweeping across his hazel eyes. "Pleasure, pure and simple. No guilt. Just something that makes you happy. I think you don't do that often enough."

She swallowed and looked away.

No one had ever said anything like that to her before. She'd always worked so hard, always striving to meet her goals, to achieve, to be the best.

Even though she knew, beyond a shadow of a doubt, that she'd never be more than she was right at that moment.

Chapter Twelve

In the days following the symphony fund-raiser, Lily attempted to put the date with Shane into perspective. He'd turned a typical foundation event into something memorable, but that didn't mean she should read more into it than that.

They'd had fun. Sitting in the ice cream parlor in a couture gown and full makeup had been a hoot. He'd gotten her to laugh, to relax, and even made her feel good about herself.

Despite Lily's worry, Marisa hadn't commented on her absence. The most important part of the evening was greeting everyone as the party got underway, and Lily supposed that since she'd been there for that, her mother was choosing to ignore her early departure.

Harp had called a couple of days ago, dropping an unsubtle hint that she didn't want to go back to teaching come March, and would be delighted if Lily came to her senses and agreed to take on a design project with her and Dani.

Lily had brushed it off, but then she'd accidentally mentioned the work she was doing for Shane.

Within minutes of hanging up with Harp, Dani had called, eager for all the details. Lily had to admit she was having more fun helping Shane than she'd expected. Seeing the interior of Dolly's house come together gave her a satisfaction that teaching alone simply couldn't bring.

But a favor for a friend was one thing. Going pro was a different animal entirely.

AS FAR AS Shane was concerned, gray was gray was gray, morning, noon and night. But Lily told him this was not the case and since he'd asked for her advice, he figured he ought to at least hear her out.

However, she seemed more interested in watching him play with Valentine than in evaluating the painted areas.

She stood with her arms crossed over her abdomen, her face a study in deliberate carelessness. She was gnawing on something.

"You look mad," he commented, taking the rope toy from Valentine and tossing it again. "Not at me, I hope. If it ends in violence, the courts will call it premeditated."

She frowned and huffed. "I'm not mad."

"Let's see. Closed body language. Frowning. Vehement denial. You're definitely mad. And I don't think it's because there are three squares, all the exact same color, with different names painted on the back wall."

"Fog Mist isn't anywhere near the same as Cloudier. And don't even get me started on Gray Mist." She uncrossed her arms, rolled her shoulders back and gave him a huge, patently fake smile. "Not mad. See?"

He couldn't help but laugh. He'd been doing that more and more lately, thanks to her. It felt good.

Valentine took advantage of Shane's momentary lapse of attention and yanked the rope toy out of his hand, jerking his bad shoulder. He winced. Served him right.

Lily took the dog toy from Valentine and threw it across the hallway into the next room.

Then she crossed her arms again and watched, expectantly.

Valentine trotted back into the room, the toy in his mouth, and went straight to Shane before dropping it.

"I'm annoyed," Lily said. "Not mad. I threw that toy. He should have brought it back to me. Not you."

Shane couldn't help but smile even though he knew it was not going to help. "You're jealous."

She rolled her eyes. Then she turned back to the swatches of paint on the bare walls. "I'm not jealous of a dog."

"Maybe he just likes men better than women. Some dogs are like that."

"Don't care. Doesn't matter." She opened a fresh can, poured a dollop into a paint tray and began loading a foam roller. "But I'm the one doing the grunt work. Feeding, brushing, scooping the yard. Cleaning the carpet when he pukes. I should be the one he likes. You're like weekend daddy, bringing presents so the kids love you, but never there when they're mouthing off or having boy trouble."

She replaced the lid on the paint can, then hammered it

shut with three sharp blows, as if punctuating the end of her comment and making sure she'd say nothing more.

It didn't work.

She lifted the second pint—fifth, actually—onto the work table, pried it open. "I know it doesn't really matter. He's not my dog so it's probably better that we don't bond. But it's as if he's under a spell, with you. Like you seduced him and made him fall in love with you and now no one else exists. Unless you plan on keeping him yourself, that's a mean thing to do. You're going to break his heart."

Shane opened the door to the backyard and let Valentine outside. The dog happily leaped down and ran after a sparrow searching for seeds in the patchy grass.

He walked over to Lily, took the roller from her hand and placed it into the tray. He pulled her into his arms and waited until he felt her soften against him.

"Lily." He felt her hair against his lips, smelled the fresh citrusy scent of her shampoo. "If anyone should keep him, it's you. You're head over heels in love with that mutt. You just won't admit it."

"That was never the plan. Once school starts up again, I'll be far too busy to look after a dog." She shook her head. "He's way too much for me—you said it yourself. I had no idea what I was getting into. This was a short-term thing, a favor for a friend and I'm just trying not to screw him up too much before we can match him with his forever family."

She hadn't, he noticed, mentioned anything about her feelings for the dog.

He picked up a strand of silky hair, curled it around his index finger and tugged gently until she looked up at him.

"What?" she said.

"Liar."

Her eyes were wide, her pupils huge. He could feel her breathing quicken against his chest. The anger was gone now, replaced by a vulnerability that made him want to hold her tighter and never let her go.

"You're scared," he whispered.

"Of him, no," she said, her gaze steady on his. "Of you, maybe. A little. Yeah."

He loosened his grip. "Me?"

"This…thing between us…was supposed to be a short-term thing, too. That's what we said."

Her eyes said everything else, how they'd agreed to let Marisa think he was Lily's boyfriend, how it turned out to be easier than either of them expected, how it was just a game because he didn't know if he'd even be around a few months from now, how his life was on pause while he reevaluated everything.

"We did." But then he'd begun smiling again and now he wasn't sure why he thought he had to leave.

"We made an agreement," she continued. "You'd help me with Valentine. I'd help you with the house."

"I'd play the role of escort at your mom's parties and you'd pretend to be my girlfriend, so Gram will stay off my back."

"It was a temporary thing."

"Temporary," he agreed.

Then her eyes grew shiny. "Because it's a lot easier when you know upfront what you're dealing with. No one gets disappointed. Nobody gets hurt. No one has," she hesitated and dropped her gaze to his lips. "Expectations."

The kiss she'd given him at the orchestra fund-raiser had been a courteous, chaste embrace designed for public consumption. But the way she looked at him now made him hungry for something more, something deeper, private, a promise, rather than a performance.

If he'd won that bet, he wouldn't have settled for a little kiss on the cheek, that's for sure.

But he hadn't. And that was good. He was starting to feel things he had no right feeling. Neither of them needed complications. They'd said that right from the beginning.

She took in a breath and gently pushed herself away. "Good." She straightened her shirt front and shook her hair away from her face. "I just wanted to make sure we were still both on the same page. Now, the light has shifted enough. Let's take another look."

She drew him to the wall where the slanting afternoon sun touched its rays. The color he'd chosen looked like something you'd use to decorate a little boy's bedroom.

"Trust me," she said, cocking an eyebrow at him. "You don't want baby blue throughout the main floor."

"Okay," he admitted. "You were right."

She pointed to the rest of the patches of gray paint, talking about the subtleties of pink undertones and violet hues and charcoal base notes.

"You sound like a sommelier. I'm looking for gray paint, not a wine pairing."

She pursed her lips and shook her head. "What you surround yourself with affects you in ways you aren't even aware of, Shane. Subtleties are important. You keep telling me that dogs are such careful observers of body language that they can pick up on the slightest mood changes, maybe before we're even aware of it ourselves. It's the same with space and light and color."

He knew she was right. But he also had the sense that she was trying to tell him something that he just couldn't quite hear. Maybe he was deaf, as well as blind.

Chapter Thirteen

THEY'D GOTTEN A lot done in the last week and a half, Shane noticed. He'd spent Tuesday morning installing baseboards while Lily continued painting. It wasn't just her eye for color that impressed him. She was meticulous with the brush and roller, leaving no paint lines, even when cutting in corners.

They took turns checking on Valentine, who amused himself in the backyard, exploring, digging and sometimes just running with pure joy. His anxiety over the collar had eased considerably. His recall was improving, though it helped to have hot dogs on hand.

In the afternoon, Shane took Valentine through his meager, elementary agility steps.

Lily watched from the deck and when the dog leaped two jumps in succession, off leash, she jumped down to join them, clapping her hands. "Brilliant, both of you!" She threw her arms around Shane. "What a wonderful surprise!"

His hands came up to her back of their own accord and for a moment, he allowed himself the pleasure of simply holding her.

"Whoa," he said. "If you're this pleased now, what will

you do when you see him walk the teeter-totter?"

She pulled back, her eyes wide. "No. You didn't teach him that."

"Not yet," he admitted. "And I probably won't. The shelter adoption event is coming soon and we've got more important things to worry about."

"Like the digging issue?"

He followed her gaze to see Valentine, head down in Gram's garden, dirt flying. "Valentine!"

The dog looked up, then returned to his digging.

"And the recall," Shane said, reaching for the bag of treats.

"He'll get there," Lily said. "But a trick like going over those jumps is just what Ariel wanted. I can just imagine you showing him off for a crowd of adoring fans. Our Valentine will have people lining up to adopt him."

She pressed her clasped hands against her chin and sighed.

"Feeling a little ambivalent about letting him go?" Shane sat down on the grass. His shoulder was bothering him. It was good to take a break, but he'd hoped to finish the baseboards and only had the entry and the powder room left.

Lily shook her head. "As long as he goes to a great home, I'll be okay." She looked at him sideways. "You sure you won't reconsider?"

He just laughed.

She had no idea how much working with Valentine had meant to him. Memories of Titan no longer ached with the same intensity.

But keeping the dog? No way.

At about five, Gram arrived with a bottle of wine, a six-pack of beer and several friends, and they toasted to the new, improved color scheme.

"Your girlfriend knows her stuff," Gram said.

"That she does," Shane replied, exchanging a smile with Lily.

"Here's to the girlfriend," chorused Gram's pals.

Later, after the friends had left and Lily was preparing to go home, Gram stopped her.

"Stay," she said. "Shane's getting pizza for supper."

"I am?" Shane looked up from his toolbox.

Gram pointed to the door. "You are."

When he returned, he found Lily and Gram curled up in the last room not currently under tarps, which happened to be his bedroom, their eyes glued to the screen.

"Quiet," Gram said. "It's starting." She turned her attention back to the television. "How does that guy keep getting a rose? He's dumber than a box of rocks."

Tuesday. Right. *Bachelorette* night.

Lily lifted a glass of wine to her lips. "He's pretty. That counts for a lot on TV."

"No amount of pretty is worth that much dumb." Gram waved him into the room. "Now here's a born winner, Lily. If you hadn't come along when you did, this boy of mine would be breaking hearts on national television."

Lily looked up at him, a smile in her eyes. "I heard."

That smile punched him in the gut. She looked so comfortable sitting there next to Gram, completely at ease in the disarray, her plaid work shirt rumpled and spattered with dried paint. She didn't have a stitch of makeup on and her hair was gathered up in her usual messy bun, yet the flickering light cast an unlikely glow of serenity that was even lovelier for being unexpected.

"Come on in and bring the pizza," Gram said, shifting to make room on the daybed for him.

Lily patted the seat beside her. "There's plenty of room."

He shrugged off his jacket and tossed it onto a chair. "Where's Val?"

Lily nodded toward the closet, where the dog was sacked out on a pile of Shane's laundry, snoring loudly. "He got into something in the garden when he was digging—"

"Potatoes," Gram said. "I must have missed a few when I harvested last fall."

"—And threw up three times while you were gone. All outside, thank goodness. He's been sleeping since."

He passed the pizza box to Gram. Poor mutt must be feeling rough if the smell of pepperoni didn't wake him up.

"Remind me, which paint color did we end up going with?" Shane slid onto the daybed next to Lily. The mattress beneath him was warm from her body, the whole scene unsettlingly cozy.

"Fog Mist," Lily said, lifting a slice of pizza to her mouth.

"Why bother telling him?" Gram said. "He thinks they

all look the same."

"Hey." Shane leaned forward, peering past Lily at his grandmother. "I thought you were on my side."

"Shh," Gram said. "Commercial's over."

Shane ate quietly while the two of them whispered back and forth as the host of the show called participants to receive the coveted flower that would keep them on for another episode.

He felt like he'd accidentally missed an episode of his own life and that it had gone on without him, with Lily slipping into a role he hadn't even realized was waiting for her.

She handed him the bowl of popcorn Gram had made during the ad break and shifted position, nestling comfortably against his shoulder.

It felt good.

Too good.

Soon, Valentine would go to a new home, Gram's home would go to a new family, he and Lily would have a sad but civil breakup to report to their respective families, and everything would go back to normal.

They hadn't discussed it directly, but of course that's what would happen. They both knew this wasn't real.

A new dread took seed in the pit of his stomach. Gram wouldn't be happy about that. But when he'd made that glib, thoughtless suggestion, he'd never expected his grandmother to get to know Lily, let alone become attached to her.

Now, with a little time on his side, Shane wondered how he and Tanya had stayed together as long as they did. She'd never have tolerated the kind of mess he was currently living in, let alone the vagueness of his future. He suspected that what she loved most about him was that he was a police officer with a secure, respectable job. And he'd loved being loved, hadn't thought much deeper than that.

Once he no longer wore the uniform, once his future was messy and painful and uncertain, their love had disappeared.

He and Tanya would never have made each other happy.

"Want a sip?" Lily held out her glass.

Her offer implied a closeness that sent warmth curling deep in his gut. When he took the glass from her, his fingers brushed hers. He was exquisitely aware of the length of Lily's thigh pressed against his.

"Thanks," he said.

"You two are so cute." Gram gave a little quiver of delight. Then a wide smile came over her face. She clapped her hands to her breast as inspiration struck.

Shane knew what she was going to say before she even opened her mouth, but he had no time to stop her.

"Lily! You're coming to the ceremony with us, aren't you?"

Lily's eyebrows rose. She gulped. Her quick side-eyed glance looked strangely guilty. "Ceremony?"

But if anyone should feel guilty, it was him and Gram lost no time making sure he knew it.

"Shane. You didn't tell her?" She leaned closer to Lily.

"He's being honored for his service. He was injured in the line of duty, you know. Apprehending a criminal. And poor, dear Titan—"

"Gram." The word felt like glass in his throat. He hadn't mentioned Titan to Lily. She wouldn't appreciate learning about him like this.

"His dog," she went on, ignoring him. "That dear creature saved Shane's life, did he tell you that?"

Lily finished her mouthful of pizza, swallowed, and wiped her mouth. "He mentioned how he got hurt. Nothing about a ceremony, though." She took a breath, like she had more to say, then pressed her lips shut.

"It's a huge honor and so well deserved," Gram said.

Shane took the pizza box and got off the bed. "It's not just about me. Other officers are getting awards, too."

"He's so modest, my boy. But you should see him in his red serge." Gram clucked. "So handsome."

"Red serge," Lily murmured. "A Mountie, then."

"It's no big deal. I doubt there are any tickets left." He lifted her wineglass, tossed back the last mouthful. "It's past the deadline. Sorry."

This sham was growing out of proportion, mushrooming like a bomb, promising the same kind of devastation in its wake.

"Don't be ridiculous." Gram was like a snowplow, relentless in her task. "They'll give you another ticket. Yvonne's dying to meet the new girlfriend."

"Yvonne?" Lily said.

Shane groaned aloud. "My mom."

"She's going to love you!" Gram clapped her hands, the deal done, as far as she was concerned. "Now you can share this with us. We're so excited to see our boy, a true hero, just like his father before him."

Her voice caught on the sharp edge of memory and a slice of it went through Shane as well. His father had been the kind of man honors like these were meant for.

Not him.

He hazarded a glance at Lily but couldn't read her expression.

"I'd be happy to attend," she said, "but it might be better with just family. We haven't known each other that long, after all. It's up to Shane."

Gram looked taken aback. Her expression turned dark. "I know he's not given to expressing himself, but I hope you understand the importance of your place in his life."

"Gram," Shane said.

"No," she continued, holding up a hand. "Let me talk. Even if what you and Lily have is merely a, what do they call it these days, friends with benefits situation—"

"Gram!" If only she knew how far from the truth that was.

Lily made a small sound that could have been a laugh, a hiccup or the indication that her last bite of pizza had gone down the wrong way. He'd prefer choking, himself, to continuing this conversation, but no such luck.

Gram glared at him. "Let me finish. Now, I'm not minimizing the value of—" she cleared her throat "—the benefits. However, friends support one another, and this will be a time when you're going to need her emotional sustenance as much as her—"

"Oh my God, Gram, boundaries." Shane lifted his eyes to the ceiling, wishing it would cave in and crush him.

"Boundaries, shmoundaries. A life doesn't belong only to one person. It's the job of those who love you to set you straight when they think you need it." She sniffed. "There's nothing new under the sun, sonny boy. However you designate your 'friendship' with Lily, I think her presence would be helpful to you."

"Dolly." Lily put her hand on the older woman's arm. "It's Shane's decision."

It took a great deal to cut off Shane's gram when she got on a roll, but somehow, Lily Garner put enough into those few words to make her mouth snap shut like a hinged gate in a windstorm.

"Time for me and Valentine to head home," Lily continued. "Thanks for the pizza, Shane. And thanks for the popcorn and wine, Dolly. I'll come back tomorrow morning, Shane. You can work with the dog while I do a second coat in the hall."

She put the sleepy dog into his harness and led him out of the room.

"Don't forget to check about the tickets," Gram called as Shane walked Lily to the front porch.

"I don't know what got into her," he said, stuffing his

hands into his pockets "Part of me thinks she's trying to trip us up."

"She does seem pretty wily."

He scuffed his feet on the porch. Then he huffed out a breath. "I don't...talk about my dog."

"It's okay. I already knew. Ariel told me about Titan."

He lifted his gaze to hers. "She did?"

Lily nodded. "Since you hadn't said anything, I figured it was a painful subject. But it explained why you're so good with Valentine."

"Who else knows?"

Lily gave him a curious look. "Lots of people, probably. You're a hero, Shane. Titan's a hero. And now you're getting an award. Seems like the sort of thing that might have come up in conversation. Aren't you excited?"

He winced. "I'm trying not to think about it."

"That's pretty clear." She bent down and patted Valentine. "It's quite something, to be recognized like that. You must be proud."

"Sure, real proud." Without thinking, he lifted his bad shoulder, then stopped when he realized what he was doing. "It's not a day I like to relive, that's all. I'm fine. Retired. Moving on with my life. I don't want to talk about it."

"I'd never have guessed." She gave him a wry smile. Something in her demeanor told him that she understood more than he realized. "You don't have a choice about this thing, do you?"

He shook his head. "Gram would never forgive me if I

blew it off."

"Having you at the symphony fund-raiser helped me," she said simply. "Maybe I can return the favor. But it's up to you. Whatever you want."

He did not see any reason to celebrate the worst moment of his life. The award would only perpetuate the festering myth of his supposed heroism, a charade he didn't want Lily to witness.

Because she might see through it, to the truth.

"Gram will never forgive me if I don't invite you."

Lily laughed and touched his hand. "Is that the best you can do? Because buddy, I've got to tell you, if I really was your girlfriend, I'd be pissed."

He felt the warmth from her fingers travel up, settle into the wounded area in his chest and spread, like the cracks in a winter pond.

Her laughter nudged an answering lightness in him and a chuckle rose.

"Lucky for you then that you aren't." He laced her fingers into his and turned to face her. "Lily Garner, would you do me the honor of joining me in an unavoidable evening of misery?"

"I'd love to." Her laugh was a moth lifting off a moonbeam. "What's another night of misery between friends?"

CHAPTER FOURTEEN

SHANE WALKED THROUGH the park, enjoying the thin winter sunshine, the light breeze and the sound of river water trickling, far below. He'd taken Lily's advice and gone for another physical therapy session on his shoulder. The rehab center was within a comfortable walking distance and the time outside always cleared his head.

The grueling session had left him tired and sore again, but it wasn't the acute discomfort like he'd had at the beginning. This was the kind of pain he'd come to associate with healing.

He'd come a long way since he'd first arrived at Gram's. His shoulder was improving, slowly but surely. He was starting to believe that the house would be ready to list by the end of winter. There was still much to do, but they were making good progress. Lily was shockingly good with a set of tools.

Not many women owned their own tool belts.

Or looked so good wearing them.

He whistled at a squirrel that scolded him from a stump. Walking under the peaceful evergreen canopy in the middle of the afternoon, like he didn't have a care in the world, was pure pleasure.

Nothing guilty about it.

He ached for Lily, for the pleasure she denied herself in hopes of pleasing her mother.

Shane was lucky. His parents had been strict, but there was never any question that they'd loved their children wholeheartedly, unconditionally. Even during adolescence, when he and his brother went about pulling pranks and pushing boundaries, Dad had reined them in without ever making them question his love.

If he'd have lived…

No. There was no point in going there. He knew his dad would be proud of him, joining the RCMP, becoming a dog handler.

But now he had no job, no dog, no purpose. What would Dad have said about that?

Same thing he'd said when Shane was struggling with any one of the minor tragedies of youth:

"You're tougher than this, Son. You've got everything you need inside yourself to get through this and I know you will. One way or another. I believe in you."

Had Lily heard that message enough times from her dad before he died? Had she ever heard it from Marisa?

A shout and sudden scuffle behind him made him turn, just in time to avoid being bowled over by Valentine.

"Hey, boy," he said, reaching out to snag the collar. "Did you get away on Lily again?"

Lily arrived a moment later, panting and red cheeked.

"He never comes when I call," she said, gasping for breath. "He knows his name. He just doesn't care. I'm gonna kill him."

"No, you're not," Shane said with a laugh. "You love him. Admit it."

She threw him a dirty look. "Wouldn't matter if I did. He's got a big fat doggy man-crush on you."

"You love him. Your feelings just are hurt because he's chosen me to be his person."

Instantly he knew he'd said the wrong thing.

Her face lit up. "You noticed! I'm so glad. Shane, Ariel and I think you should adopt Valentine."

He took a step backward. "Whoa, good try, no thank you."

Her expression faded. "But you like him. And he likes you."

And that was reason enough, but she wouldn't understand.

"He'll find another person. In the meantime, I can help you work on that recall."

"How? Every time I let him off the leash for some exercise, he finds a trail and he's gone. I can't call him back for love or money. Or treats."

He squatted down and let the dog lick his chin. "Let's practice something I tried the day we first met. Do you remember?"

She looked at him through her lashes. "I remember. You made fun of my outfit."

He grinned. "I made fun of the dog's outfit. You looked spectacular."

Her windblown hair, the scratch on her cheek. The softness of her skin. He'd thought of that day so many times.

"Oh." She looked flustered. "What did you want to try?"

He wanted to try a lot of things, starting off with getting a proper kiss from her.

But first things first.

He pointed down the path. "You walk out that way, while I give him some love. You've got treats with you?"

She nodded.

"Good." He waited until she was about twenty feet away. Then he straightened up and ignored the dog. "Start running."

"What?"

"Run!"

She took off. After a brief look up at Shane, Valentine galloped after Lily.

"Now, stop and reward."

Lily bent down and ruffled his ears, heaping words of praise on the overjoyed dog.

"Now stop giving him attention," Shane called, and started running.

Valentine looked between the two of them in confusion for a moment, and then once more chased after the moving target.

They ran back and forth like this several times, praising and rewarding Valentine's participation.

Then they slowed to a jog. Valentine recognized the game.

"Now," Shane instructed, "call his name and walk away."

"Valentine, come." She said it with authority and excitement and the dog responded, just as he had when she was running.

"Good boy!" she praised. She looked up at Shane. "It worked. That's amazing!"

"It's not foolproof, by any means," he cautioned. "But we created a situation in which he's coming to you voluntarily. We'll need to practice regularly, so he associates the behavior and will do it even when distracted."

Her eyes were shining. To know that he'd put that look on her face made him feel, for a moment, like a million bucks, like Superman, Ryan Reynolds and Ryan Gosling all rolled into one.

Like the hero people said he was.

LILY COULD HAVE skipped like a schoolgirl all the way home. "Who's a good boy?" she said in a crooning voice.

At her side, Valentine looked up, his tail wagging. He wasn't even pulling at the leash anymore. Their recall practice had tuckered him out.

She, on the other hand, felt high on success. Valentine had obeyed, willingly, eagerly, and his delight at her praise warmed her heart. He so desperately wanted to please her.

"That's right," she said. "You're a good boy. You're the best boy."

Soon, a child would be able to walk him.

He'd be a good family dog, ready to start his new life in a loving home. Just as they'd planned.

The glow faded.

Giving him up wasn't going to be easy. They'd have to make sure his new owners were committed to working hard with him. Maybe she and Shane could help with the transition, even do some training sessions with them.

No, she thought. The dog was going to be confused enough, going to yet another home. He'd need a clean break, if he was to bond the way she wanted him to. The way he deserved.

If only Shane would keep him, she thought again. Then she'd still get to visit him.

Except, Shane had never mentioned what he'd be doing once Dolly's house was sold.

Her steps slowed, her excitement fading. Would he leave town, go back to his friends and family in Prince George? Look for another construction job here?

Her cell phone buzzed. She fished it out of her pocket and looked at the screen. Marisa's face smiled back at her.

"Hello, Mom," she said.

"Darling, I hope I'm not interrupting another—" she cleared her throat delicately "—training session."

"Ha, ha. We just finished. Take that whatever way you like." Then she felt bad for goading her mother. "Was there something you needed?"

Marisa paused. "Can't a mother call up her daughter just to talk?"

Lily opened the gate and walked up to her front door. "Sure, of course." She let herself in, then stooped down to free Valentine from the leash. He immediately loped to the water dish for a long drink.

Her mother sounded different and she couldn't quite put her finger on why.

"How's Sebastian?" She hung the leash on the peg by the door.

"He sends his love." Another pause. Then she continued, her words coming out in a rush. "I hope you know, Lily, how much I appreciate everything you've done for me recently, especially since you'd rather be pursuing your own interests."

Lily opened her mouth to protest but Marisa didn't give her a chance.

"We may not have found your ideal place in the Kovac Foundation yet, but darling we will. And you'll be just as passionate about our work as I am."

Sitting down at the kitchen table, Lily chose her words carefully. "I know how much the foundation means to you, Mom," she began. "But I'll never be passionate about calling vendors, taping up streamers and making emergency trips to the liquor store when the booze runs low."

"You do so much more than that, Lily!" Marisa sounded shocked. "You're a social facilitator. You have no idea how important that is in the world of philanthropy. The Kovac Foundation supports so many worthy causes. Our endorsement brings other donors to the table, but they don't open their wallets until they trust us, and they don't trust us until they're comfortable. We don't just throw parties, dear. We help people discover their own generosity."

Guilt stabbed her again. It's not like her mother was blowing the family fortune selfishly. The Kovac Foundation had done so much good, for so many people. Marisa enjoyed herself in the process. So what?

"Radisson is quite a catch, dear," Marisa was saying.

The guilt disappeared. "Mom. We've been over this."

"I'm sure Chad would forgive you as well, if you asked. And as far as that Shane person goes, I know you only invited him to annoy me. Next time you can save us all the discomfort and accompany the guest I intend for you."

Marisa had pushed too far.

"Shane might not be a knight in shining armor," she said, "but he's a hell of a sight better than either of those two schmucks."

"Lily!"

"Bye, Mom." Lily ended the call and looked out the window. She still had her jacket on. "Come on, Valentine. We're going back outside, for me, this time."

For once, he seemed to get the message she conveyed through the leash. This was not a time for frivolity. She headed down the sidewalk at an almost jog, eager to clear her mind before she started crying.

She was a grown woman, for heaven's sake. How was it that one conversation with her mother could still reduce her to tears? When would she be over this?

They paused at the intersection and waited for the light to turn. "Valentine, sit."

He looked up at her and, to her great amazement, he promptly dropped his butt and sat. His angle was a bit wonky, no military precision there, but he sat.

On command.

"Good boy, Valentine!" She bent down and rubbed his ears. He immediately leaped up and bonked her head with his own bony skull.

"Ouch!" She was smiling through her tears though, as she dug in her pocket for the treat he so richly deserved.

Maybe she wasn't a failure at dog training, after all. Maybe there was hope for him. Maybe, with a bit more patience and work, and a little more coaching from Shane, this poor unwanted dog would finally attract his forever family.

He wasn't a loser any more than she was. He just needed to find his audience.

CHAPTER FIFTEEN

"WELCOME TO THIS special night honoring the men and women who serve at the Maple Grove detachment of the Royal Canadian Mounted Police." Mayor Greg Conrad smiled at the small crowd seated in the auditorium.

Lily sat next to Dolly. Yvonne Bowman, Shane's mother, was next to Dolly, her expression tense, her posture tight.

They'd met outside the building and had only a moment to chat before being ushered inside for the ceremony. Lily agreed with Dolly that Shane's mother was a lovely woman. But this evening held a great deal of emotional significance for them both. A part of Lily felt like she was intruding on a private event.

But a bigger part knew that however the women felt, Shane's feelings were more intense. She was here to support him, whatever that meant.

At the signal, the officers marched into the auditorium. When Shane appeared, Lily's hand went to her mouth. Her breath caught in her throat.

He was a handsome man in his paint-stained jeans and shirts.

Today, in the high-collared scarlet tunic and midnight-blue breeches of RCMP fame, he was stunning. Oxblood riding boots and a wide, flat-brimmed hat completed the picture.

Someone from the front came to the mic and the ceremony began but Lily barely heard them.

She couldn't take her eyes off Shane. He stood so straight and tall, so stern and unbending. His lips were compressed to a thin white line and he stared unblinkingly at something far beyond everyone in the room.

One by one, officers were named. They came forward and were given a plaque, a pin or a medal. The commissioner gave a brief description of the event for which they were being recognized.

So many brave men and women.

"Sergeant Shane Bowman," the commissioner announced.

Shane stepped forward, his face blank, like a wall of granite.

"On the night of November fourteen," said the host, reading from his notes, "Sergeant Bowman intercepted a robbery in progress. The assailant was armed with a knife and a gun and while carrying out his duty, Sergeant Bowman was shot three times."

Three times, Lily thought. She hadn't heard about that.

"His partner, Police Service Dog Titan, stopped the fourth bullet and later died of his injuries. Despite their wounds, Sergeant Bowman and PSD Titan prevented the suspect from completing his objective. Today, we recognize this outstanding service. Thank you, Sergeant Bowman."

Shane removed his hat and bent his head as the commissioner placed a silver medallion around his neck.

Not a single person in the audience would have seen him shaking, she thought. His posture gave away nothing. His expression remained impassive. He barely blinked.

But Lily felt the electric energy flowing off him as if there was a line connecting them. He didn't talk about Titan. He didn't allow anyone else to talk about him. The night he'd lost his partner was not one to celebrate, she knew.

And yet he was here, accepting his due.

When the formalities were over, she hung back, unsure as to what her role was or what he needed from her.

Shane stood in the line, shaking hands and accepting with grace the words of comfort, condolence and encouragement that came to him over and over.

Maybe she'd imagined the depth of his emotion. He seemed fine now.

Finally, the line ended, and the last person continued to the room beyond, where refreshments were being served. Shane looked behind him and, seeing the empty room, he exhaled. He lifted his head, as if suddenly awakening to his surroundings. His face relaxed but in place of the stoic sternness, came exhaustion and grief, haunting and harsh. When his eyes landed on hers, she felt it again, the pain radiating from him.

Lily took a step toward him. Rows and rows of empty

seats stood between them. She made another tentative movement in his direction. Did he want comfort? Did he want to be alone? Was there any comfort to be given?

She'd had no idea what he'd gone through on the night he'd lost his dog. No idea of the pain, both physical and emotional, he'd been dealing with since then. He hid it well.

Only now, at this moment, under the bright lights of the stage could she see just how much it had cost him.

He swallowed, his throat jerking with the effort, and took a stumbling step toward the low stairs leading off the stage.

Lily rushed toward him, capturing his hands in hers.

"It's okay," she whispered. "I've got you."

He yanked her to his chest, crushing her against his uniform.

She could feel his strong arms shaking, quaking. She wished she could take some of his pain from him, wished that she could take the memories of fear and anguish and tuck them away, somewhere safe, for when he was ready for them. For now, he needed the good memories, the ones of him and Titan playing, working, winning, loving.

HE LEANED AGAINST the wall and pulled harsh, gulping breaths deep into his lungs. "I'm fine," he gasped, hoping he'd managed to get out of sight before falling apart. "I just need some air."

Blood thrummed against his eardrums. His fingers tingled. He couldn't feel his legs and feared they would buckle beneath him. At the same time, he imagined himself above, observing the small room from a corner in the ceiling, while he came undone.

And Lily watched.

Humiliation scorched through him. "I'll meet you in the reception hall. Give me a minute, okay?"

"What kind of fake girlfriend would I be if I abandoned you in your moment of need? Besides, you've seen me at my worst. This just levels the playing field."

Her words were soft and light but there was a tremor in her voice.

She had a vise grip on his upper arm, holding him steady. With the other hand, she rubbed firm wide circles on his back. He put his mind's eye on the spiral movements and soon felt himself pull up from the brink.

He knew what disgust looked like when it was masked with concern. The sound of that thin veneer cracking on the face of someone he cared about still echoed like a gunshot.

He hung his head. His breathing was coming easier now, but adrenaline left him shaky with a metallic taste on his tongue. He should never have allowed her to come. He should have predicted this.

"Hey," Lily said. "Whatever you're thinking, stop it."

He shook his head. "You've no idea what I'm thinking."

"Wanna bet?" She squeezed his arm. "You started hyperventilating as soon as they got to you."

He closed his eyes, knowing she was right. Wondering who else had noticed. "It was that obvious?"

"Everyone was too busy thinking about what an amazing thing you did. Their eyes were on the speaker." She shook her head. "But I was watching you, Shane. I had a feeling. That's why I know that you're right back there, in that day. Thinking about the bullet, the fear. Titan."

He couldn't meet her gaze. She'd been watching him. Watching out for him.

The muscles in his chest loosened. She wasn't scared off by his weakness; she'd anticipated it, been ready for it.

She hadn't run away.

Footsteps sounded from the hallway around the corner.

"Shane?"

He jerked his head toward the door. "It's my mom," he whispered.

She was like a spaniel on the trail of her wounded son. He couldn't let her see him like this.

"Shane, are you all right?"

Before he could think of an explanation, Lily swung around to face him, grabbed his face in both hands and pulled him close.

"Go with me," she whispered. Then she kissed him. Hard.

Her lips hijacked his brain, took over the controls and brought the wheeling cargo of memory up from its nosedive. Instantly, he returned fully to his body, every skin cell alive and tingling, every nerve dancing.

She moved her hands from his face to link them behind his neck, pressing her soft body into him, stroking the hair at his nape. She nibbled and tasted as if he was the feast she'd been saving her appetite for. Her breath was sweet and hot on his face, her mouth soft, her questing tongue tasting of pure fresh water and joy.

She made a small sound in the back of her throat, a murmur or a moan, and it went straight through him. He cupped the back of her head in his palm, pulling her closer, as if he wanted to devour her. He pressed her against the wall and she lifted one knee and brought it against his thigh, pushing the base of her body against his aching groin.

Delicious. Irresistible. Her unbridled desire lit an answering flame in him. Damn, he hadn't expected her to be such a great actor. This was going to complicate things.

Unless she wasn't acting.

The door swung open.

"Oh! My goodness."

He pulled his head away from Lily and turned to see his mother, blinking.

"Mom." He searched his brain for something else to say. His senses felt blurred and exquisitely acute at the same time. Emotional whiplash, he thought.

"Oops. You caught us." Lily's eyes sparkled. Her cheeks were bright pink, her lips swollen and moist. She twined her fingers with Shane's and glanced up at him, smiling mischievously. "It's the first time I've seen your son in uniform. I guess I got a little carried away."

"I can understand that." Yvonne smiled but there were anxious lines at the corners of her eyes. "Everything okay, Shane?"

No.

Yes.

Of course his mother was worried. She knew him too well. That's why he hadn't wanted her to come. In the weeks and months after the shooting, she'd been there for him, tough as nails, knowing that tenderness would have broken him. Still, she'd watched him pull away, fight the temptation to sink into pain and despair. She'd done everything in her power to bring him back to himself, to keep herself together for his sake because if she gave in to her own rage and fear, she'd be no good to her son.

He felt warmth rising on his neck. "Considering you just walked in on me making out with my girl, sure."

His stomach twisted at the lie, but it was a damn sight better than her walking in on him freaking out about an event he should be long over.

And Lily wasn't his girl.

But he kept her hand in his, as if she was. It felt…right.

Lily straightened her sweater and smoothed her hair. "Now that this awkward moment has passed, can we all agree to never mention it again?"

Yvonne looked upward. "Mention what? The fudge brownies waiting out in the hall?"

"Fudge brownies?" Lily tugged on Shane's hand. "Come on. Those babies are going to go fast."

Shane followed the two women, the one who'd known him his whole life and would do anything for him, and the one who barely knew him, but found the perfect moment to do exactly what he needed.

No, he wasn't okay. He was in big, big trouble.

Chapter Sixteen

THEY LEFT AS soon as was socially acceptable, Shane dropping her off at her door and parking down the street at his own place. He'd been quieter than usual in the car and neither of them mentioned the kiss.

Should she have apologized?

Or should she have kissed him again, for real, this time?

Lily paused, her hand on the gate, listening across the misty night air for the soft click of his car door closing, for his footsteps walking up the rain-slicked sidewalk to his front door.

Then she sighed and lowered herself to the swing that hung in the sheltered porch, tucked one leg up in front of her and let her head fall back. The languid back-and-forth motion unwound the tension in her shoulders and she allowed herself to remember the sensation of his lips on hers, his hard flesh beneath her fingers, against her body.

The kiss had been a spur-of-the-moment improvisation, meant to distract Yvonne, to redirect her attention and convince her that her worry was misplaced.

Lily could have done a million other things: pretended to be taking something out of his eye. Pretended to be overwhelmed with emotion, herself, and letting Shane comfort her. Pretended to be practicing her acceptance speech for the Academy Award she'd be getting one day for all this pretending.

Instead, she'd pretended they were making out.

And there'd been nothing pretend about it.

Truth was, she *had* been overcome, seeing Shane up there. The blank expression on his face as they'd recited the bare facts about the night that had ended his career had struck her harder than if he'd been weeping. Shane looked like he'd been carved from granite, like the shattered bone and muscle and dreams had happened to someone else, like the wounded heart and mind had been a mirage, a dream, a story conjured up by those in need of a hero to worship.

And when that granite had cracked in the hallway, when the mask had slipped, and he'd clutched her hand, had gripped the wall, her own heart had lurched inside her chest.

This is real, her heart said.

This is a man of honor. A man worth wanting.

A man she could love.

No! She squeezed her eyes tight against the thought.

She didn't want to want him. She couldn't want him, she'd sworn to him that she was as sick of matchmaking as he was, that all she wanted was to have one relationship unsullied by expectations and artifice. She should have stipulated something about desire, she realized now, for that was at the heart of it.

She'd so wanted to be free of the craving, the want, the

yearning aching emptiness. And with Shane, there had been no craving. It wasn't an option. They weren't trying to be anything for each other but exactly what and who they were.

Such a relief, she'd no idea.

And then she'd gone and kissed him.

She banged her forehead lightly against her knee. "You dummy. You're ruining everything."

A fake relationship didn't require fake kissing. What was next? Fake make-out sessions in the car? Fake getting naked? Fake sleeping together? Fake taking showers together?

She shuddered, imagining a line of soapy water trailing the muscled planes of his back, to his hard buttocks, his thighs and knees and calves. Was he hairy or manscaped? Hairy, she guessed, but not excessively so.

"Stop it!" She had no business imagining his body, hair or no hair.

She moaned and pressed the back of her head against the cushioned headrest. This was all her fault and, somehow, she was going to have to get herself under control before their next meeting.

They could have kept up the charade easily with an occasional bit of hand-holding. Maybe a kiss on the cheek, if someone was watching.

But that soul-searing, open-mouthed dance of tasting and touching and knowing—that wasn't part of the game.

Yes, her intentions had been pure. She'd taken the attention off Shane's momentary lapse of composure and turned it into a cute moment, a lovers' tryst. Embarrassing, but not alarming. They'd been successful enough to reassure Yvonne that her son was doing just fine.

That's all Shane had wanted, for this group of friends, co-workers, family, who all cared for him and worried for him, to know that he was okay.

Whether or not it was the truth.

Had she done him a favor then, or not? Perhaps if he still struggled with the after effects of that night, he ought to be surrounded by those who knew him best.

She sighed and got out of the basket swing. Inside, Valentine greeted her with soft whines and head nudges indicating an urgent need to visit the hedge in the backyard. He'd come a long way since she'd first brought him home. He was far better equipped now for life with a family, and that was largely due to Shane's assistance.

She gave Valentine a bedtime snack and padded about the house closing blinds and turning off lights, wishing she could turn off her mind as easily. She felt as if every new thing she'd learned about Shane in the past few hours had only triggered a landslide of new questions.

For instance, his deflection about his future. Once the construction on Gram's house was completed, and the house sold, what would he do? Where would he go?

None of his fellow officers at the reception, she recalled, had asked Shane about returning to the force. After hearing the details about the shooting and seeing the expressions on the faces of those involved, she couldn't help but hope Shane was indeed out of it. He had been a skilled and passionate policeman; that was obvious. But was that passion worth risking his life for?

Yvonne and Dolly had stayed behind, being well acquainted with many of the other officers and their families, and happy for the opportunity to catch up.

How did military and law enforcement spouses live with that horrible potential? Each time they saw their loved one off to work, they did it with the knowledge that this shift, this deployment could be the one that held a tragedy, that this goodbye could be the last one for all time.

Lily couldn't imagine it. She couldn't imagine the pain of seeing him fighting for his life, of facing the fact that she could lose him, that they could lose each other.

Of course, everyone on the planet awoke each day with no guarantee of surviving to the night. Accidents happened all the time, to even the most careful. Health-conscious athletes were struck by cancer, a piece of meat could lodge in a baby's windpipe, a man in the prime of life could have a massive heart attack.

Her throat tightened unbearably. Her father had survived, the first time. And upon his recovery, his old life no longer fit him. He'd grabbed his second chance with both hands and set out to make the most of it, unburdened by family responsibility.

He'd left them.

Left her.

And then he'd died, without them.

She stared into her own eyes as she removed her makeup

at the bathroom vanity. Marisa had married again, after a time, though it seemed to Lily to be a cautious investment on both sides, rather than an all-in gamble. Sara hadn't suffered any doubts, choosing the path predetermined for her, happy with a conventional future.

But the wheel of fortune hadn't stopped on a winning number for Lily. The bouncing marble never landed where she'd laid her bet and only when she'd given up the game had she found any relief.

But it didn't last.

Valentine flopped onto the carpet beside her bed as she removed her makeup and changed into her sleep shirt. Before turning out the light, she folded herself down onto the floor beside him.

"You're a good boy, Val." Tears sprang to her eyes. There were no guarantees, in anything. Life and love were capricious, but you could always count on a dog to make you smile.

He thumped his tail and pawed at her.

She rubbed his belly, which earned her deep moans of appreciation. "A very good boy."

He blinked up at her, his dark eyes liquid with adoration, and for the first time, she realized that her little house would be very quiet again once he was gone.

Perhaps…

No.

She shook her head and forced herself to look away from his pleading eyes. The same reason she wanted to get a dog was the reason it wouldn't be fair of her to get one. Shane's speculation that much of Valentine's bad behavior was due to neglect rang true to her. Dogs didn't like being alone any more than people did and when her normal schedule resumed, she'd be far too busy to keep an energetic dog happy. He'd be alone in the house for hours at a time. He'd be bored, he'd become destructive, she'd return home from work too tired to provide more than a perfunctory walk before collapsing in front of the television.

That's no life for a dog.

It didn't sound like much of a life at all. Next time, maybe she should foster a cat. If she bonded with it, there was a chance things would work out. Cats didn't mind solitude. In fact, they preferred it, right?

But would any other animal look at her the way Valentine was looking at her right now?

"Quit it," she told him. "You deserve a family. You're not supposed to make me fall in love with you."

He flipped over, twisted around and leaped to his feet, his eager expression begging her to play.

"Not helping," she said. But he wasn't giving up. Fine. She could afford a little playtime before bed. "Get your toy."

To her surprise, he stopped and looked around the room, as if he understood her words. Then, he went to the basket in the corner, pulled out a braided rope pull toy and brought it to her.

Coincidence? Must be.

"Who's a smart boy?" She rewarded him with a few

rounds of tug-of-war. She couldn't wait to tell Shane about this. Had he taught the dog this trick? Or was the retriever instinct in him all along, just waiting for the right environment to emerge?

But the idea of Valentine showing off his skills for someone else didn't give her the same excitement it used to. All she could imagine now was watching him walk away from her, into the waiting arms of someone who might or might not give him all the love he deserved.

No guarantees.

Chapter Seventeen

A FEW DAYS later, Lily met Dani and Harp at the animal shelter. The two of them had volunteered their services with the cleanup and repair of the shelter, which had touched her heart, especially since Dani's baby was beginning to get in the way.

"Hey, girlfriend," Harpreet said, giving her a hug. "I hear your fake fake boyfriend Shane is a hero."

Lily felt her cheeks color. She'd given up protesting that there was nothing between her and Shane. "Yes, he is," she agreed. "I was there for the awards ceremony."

"My fake fake husband says your fake fake boyfriend is making the rest of mankind look bad." Dani made a face. "I may have been talking him up a bit too much."

"Any progress?" Harpreet lifted her eyebrows suggestively. "You know. On the romance front?"

"Harp." Lily aimed for a breezy, don't-be-ridiculous tone. "We're friends."

Except the memory of that kiss sent even more heat to her cheeks.

Dani put her hands to her mouth. "You're lying! She's lying. Look at her face, Harp! Lily, tell us right now. What happened?"

"Nothing," she said, putting her hands over her face.

"Extreme lying," Harpreet said. "And badly, too. Must be something big."

Lily peeked between her fingers. "I kissed him."

Dani squealed. "You did? This is good, girlfriend."

"No, it's not," Lily said with a groan. "Why am I such an idiot?"

"Was it a good kiss?" Harpreet asked.

"Oh, yes," Lily sighed. "A very, very good kiss."

"What's the problem, then?" Dani massaged her baby bump.

"What's not the problem?" Lily said. "Neither of us wanted this. And even if we did, he's only here temporarily. He's got his career to figure out."

"Just like you," Harpreet put in. "Have you asked him what his plans are?"

"No," Lily admitted. "I don't think he wants to talk about it."

"Maybe he doesn't know," Dani said. "Maybe he's waiting for a sign. A reason to stay. You could make the first move, you know."

Harpreet narrowed her eyes at Lily. "You've got feelings for him, don't you?"

"No!" Lily said. Then she let her head drop. "Maybe. I think so. I wasn't supposed to! I'm not sure how it happened. But that kiss, let me tell you, did not help."

"I think," Dani said, "it was exactly what you needed.

And about time."

To Lily's relief, Ariel walked out of the building just then and greeted the three of them.

"Great news!" she said, reaching for Lily's hand. "Remember what we talked about?"

Lily glanced at her friends and nodded cautiously.

"This is top secret intel," Ariel said, lowering her voice.

Dani placed her hand on her heart. "I won't tell a soul."

"Me neither," echoed Harpreet.

"Shane's dog Titan has been chosen by the Animal Heroes Society to be inducted into the Animal Hall of Fame." She squealed and jumped up and down. "This is going to be so great! We're going to do it at the Adoption Option night, which has now been changed to a Tuxes and Tails cocktail party, and we're going all out with the Valentine's Day theme. Hearts. Love. Sharing love with animals. How animals fill our hearts. You know what I mean. Your handsome cop hero will be the star of the show." Ariel paused. "Your show."

"What?" Lily didn't know where to begin. Shane was coming to help her out with Valentine. He didn't want to relive the shooting again, in front of a bunch of strangers.

Then Ariel's words registered.

"What do you mean, my show?"

"Well," Ariel bit her lip. "That's the other thing I wanted to ask you about."

Harp and Dani suddenly looked at each other.

"We'll get started cleaning out the storage room," Dani

said.

As soon as they were gone, Lily turned to her friend, who wore a look of hopeful sheepishness that she'd come to know. And dread.

"What have you done?"

Ariel folded her hands together and blinked winningly. "I may have offered," she began, "to have you organize the event."

Lily's jaw fell open.

"And I think I accidentally dropped a couple of names, too."

"Ariel," Lily said warningly.

"It's just that she knows so many people!" Ariel protested, her words tumbling out in a flood now. "If people knew that your mother was going to be at this thing, if the Kovac Foundation was behind it, we'd have our new shelter paid for in no time."

Lily shook her head. There was no doubt that what Ariel said was true.

But there was also no doubt about Marisa Rollins's response.

"You've met my mother," she said, hoping her friend wouldn't be too disappointed. "If her friends have any interest in pets, it's the kind that live in designer bags, not scruffy homeless animals. The chances are of her coming to an animal shelter benefit? None. No chance. Sorry."

"Unless." Ariel held up her index finger. Instead of disappointment, there was an air of anticipation in her voice that made Lily think of TV lawyers about to deliver the final key piece of evidence.

"Unless what?"

"I'm not as thick as you think, my friend. Tell me. What's the one thing Marisa can't resist?"

Lily didn't have to think. "Attention."

"Right." Here it comes. "Well, then this ought to convince her. This event is going to be, as I'd hoped, televised."

Lily blinked. "Really?"

"Yes. The local cable channel is super hyped. They want to support us with, not just the adoptions, but with a special donation-matching initiative, to go toward building a new facility!"

"What!" Lily was dumbfounded. This was huge for the shelter.

"Pretty awesome, huh? So, what do you say?"

It would be great for the shelter, no doubt about it. But would her mother agree? She hadn't once set foot in the shelter and certainly wouldn't do so in front of cameras.

"Wait." Lily skewered Ariel with her eyes. "Where is thing supposed to be held? We certainly can't hold it here."

Ariel spread her hands wide. "Totally up to you! You've got carte blanche, my friend. Design us an event to remember."

"Argh!"

Would she even be able to find a venue for such an event at such short notice?

Then she straightened her shoulders. She had access to all

sorts of spaces. Marisa, as Ariel said, had friends in high places. People with property, sprawling ranch homes, horse farms, training rings, tony locations that would be suitable for dogs, but could also be made gala ready.

Then she returned to the point that bothered her the most. The one that could prove to be even more of a stickler than Marisa.

"Titan's really getting an award?"

"The Animal Heroes Society does it every year," Ariel said. "Someone nominated Titan after the RCMP award thing."

"Someone, huh?" Lily raised an eyebrow.

"Okay, it was me. But Shane's grandmother gave me the information I needed. She seems like a very nice lady."

Dolly was bound and determined to see her handsome grandson's face on television.

"I want people to recognize that the sacrifice wasn't just Shane's alone. That he'd had a wonderful partner at his side, a partner that died in the line of duty." Ariel's voice hitched. "You might think I'm being high-handed and selfish, Lily, but Titan deserves this. If it can help the shelter, too, then all the better."

Shane would hate this so much. He'd never agree to it if he knew his dog, and by association, he himself, would once more be put in the spotlight. But she also knew that he had to come to terms with Titan's death if he ever wanted to move on in his life.

"When will you tell Shane about it?"

Ariel gave a pleading grin. "I was hoping we could keep it a surprise."

For a moment, she stared at Ariel. No wonder she was so good at her job. She went from puppy-dog eyes to pit-bull tenacity, as the situation demanded.

Dogs made Shane smile. He'd resisted working with Valentine initially but once they'd started, he'd taken a real interest. He needed another dog.

He needed Valentine, she thought again.

He needed to remember that love was good, even when it hurt, or maybe, because it always entailed risk and was therefore more precious.

"You're lucky I like you," she told Ariel.

Her friend gave an ear-splitting cheer. "I knew it. You're the best. This is going to be fantastic, for everyone."

But not for Shane.

Possibly not for her either. There was a good chance Shane would see it as a betrayal.

But that was a chance she'd just have to take.

What was love without the risk of loss?

Chapter Eighteen

Some conversations simply had to take place in person.

Lily sat in her mother's front parlor, sipping orange pekoe from a bone china cup, wondering if this would be the day that Marisa finally gave up on her for good.

"Excuse me." Marisa's cup didn't even rattle against the saucer. "What did you say?"

Lily took another slow breath. "You heard me right, Mother. A Valentine's Day fund-raiser, for the animal shelter where I volunteer."

Heavily mascaraed lashes fluttered. Then Marisa gave an apologetic smile. "Darling, I know how much you love animals. It's a testament to your soft heart. I love that about you, I really do." Her smile took on a pained note, and a slight frown marred her smooth forehead. "But you know that I have a reputation to uphold. People have expectations. My endorsement implies a certain level of...quality. Culture. Animal messes don't work with tuxes and tails, darling. Surely you can understand."

It was the same message she'd received all her life. The Rollinses were about beauty, order, status, predictability.

Anything that defied that was not for them.

"You know what's cool? That's the name we're using for the fund-raiser. Tuxes and Tails." Lily crossed her arms. She'd known this is how Marisa would respond, but suddenly she was tired of hearing the same old lines. "I told Ariel that you'd say no. I told her that I held no sway with you, that if anything, my asking would only make you less likely to agree. You've proven me right, so thanks for that. But don't tell me I have to understand. I'm your child. This is important to me. Doing this would be so easy for you." Her throat thickened, and she swallowed. "A simple thing, a favor for your own daughter and you simply won't consider it. I shouldn't be hurt. I shouldn't be surprised. But we've been getting along better, and I thought, somehow, this once, maybe things would be different."

Marisa looked away. A tendon in her throat twitched but other than that, her expression was bland. "A favor for my child." She gave a small sniff, the kind of laugh you give something that has never been funny. "Everything is so simple for you, isn't it, Lily? You have no idea what it's like..."

She hesitated and for just a moment, someone else appeared behind the mask Marisa so carefully cultivated, a woman who doubted her true self so much that she hid. Lily's heart went out to that person, the mother she remembered only in fleeting snapshots from long ago. A mother who played and laughed and smiled with her whole face instead of just her mouth.

The mother who saw her, heard her, knew her.

A mother who was there.

And then she was gone, leaving the smooth-masked woman in her place.

Lily exhaled heavily. She'd wanted her mother to agree willingly but she wasn't Marisa Rollins's daughter for nothing. This was important, not just for the shelter, and for Valentine, but for Shane.

"There's going to be substantial media coverage," Lily said.

Marisa's head lifted. Her eyebrows went up.

"The Animal Heroes Society will be recognizing several outstanding acts of animal bravery on that night," Lily went on. "You may not think pets are important, but there are a lot of people who do. And those people will be at this event."

"Why didn't you mention that at the outset, darling?" Marisa was all smiles now. "This changes everything."

Of course it did. Lily pushed down the disappointment and braced herself to deliver the rest of her message. She was tired of being manipulated. It was time she decided to run her own life and it started now.

"Here's how it's going to work, Mom. We'll need a location with space for several hundred guests. Something suitable for dogs, because we'll be bringing many to circulate among the guests. A staging area as well as a podium. Plenty of parking. Someone in the horsey crowd will no doubt have a covered riding ring they'd be happy to let us use. You're going to use your substantial influence to make this happen.

Then, you're going to stir up buzz. We want this to be the most anticipated Valentine's Day event in town."

Marisa opened her mouth to protest but Lily didn't let her.

"I'll work with your tradespeople to arrange the decor, lighting, rentals, food, beverage service, everything, just as I always do. It's going to be amazing, we'll celebrate the human-animal bond and recognize some very special animals. All funds raised will go toward building a new, larger shelter, something we've needed for a long, long time."

"You've got it all worked out." Marisa's posture was stiff. "I suppose I need to start making some phone calls. I hope you don't think this high-handed attitude will work for future projects, but I understand that in this case, you may know better than I what is needed."

She was hurt; Lily could see that. And as always with Marisa, hurt turned into anger, and then withdrawal. It was time to change the pattern.

"Mom." Lily touched her mother's forearm, stilling her. "I love you. I want to keep loving you. And that's why, after this event, I'm done working for you. This work doesn't fulfill me and it's damaging us. So, I'm quitting. My friends want me to start a design firm with them. Maybe I will, maybe I won't. Point is, as long as I'm working for you, I can't entertain the possibility. I need to live my own life, Mom. I hope you can understand."

Marisa froze. Her chin went up, her shoulders back. "Sara isn't ready to return yet."

Just like Marisa to leap over Lily's news and go straight to her own concerns.

"Sara will come back part time."

"You've spoken with her?"

Lily nodded. "She's better at the party scene than I am, Mom. She's who you need here."

Marisa examined her fingernails, frowning. "Your own firm. So that wasn't just an excuse Shane made, to get you out of the symphony gala early?"

Lily smiled, remembering the fun they'd had afterward.

"I've been thinking about it for a while. He gave me a nudge."

His encouragement and the work on his house had made the idea seem possible.

"What about your teaching?"

"I'll continue that for now. I enjoy what I do, Mom. I'm a good teacher." She took a deep breath. "I'm a good designer, too. I have to try."

Marisa twisted the rings on her left hand. "You sound just like your father."

Lily's back straightened. "What does that mean?"

"Nothing." Marisa gave her head a little shake. "I assume you've done the ground work? You know what an uphill battle you'll be undertaking?"

"We know. But we've already got some clients." The board had given Dani and Harp permission to help design the new animal rescue facility. Media coverage at the fundraiser would bring attention to their fledgling business, as well as the shelter. It wasn't much. But they'd start slow.

Marisa was quiet for a while. Then she folded her hands in her lap, looked at her daughter and smiled. "I wish you every success, my dear. Now, I have a place in mind that would be perfect for your cocktail party."

CHAPTER NINETEEN

AUSTIN ACRES WAS a hobby farm near the river, owned by a pair of optometrists who, it turned out, were huge animal lovers and more than happy to host the event. Especially once Marisa Rollins made a call.

Lily had put her friends to work rather than utilize foundation employees, wherever possible. Between Harpreet, Dani and their husbands, Ariel and the shelter volunteers and Shane, they had more than enough help pulling it together.

Dani and Harp had also lent a hand getting Dolly's place completed. With their help, Lily convinced Shane that details in a house like this mattered. He reluctantly returned all the faucets, light fixtures, doorknobs, and cabinet hardware he'd purchased from Home Depot. When Harpreet showed him the vintage items they'd found at an estate sale, he admitted they'd been right.

Everything was coming together. Neither of them had mentioned the kiss. If anything, the intimacy seemed to have sent them both back to their corners, like boxers after the first round, unsure of what to expect next.

Shane regretted it; she was certain. Why else would he

pull away from her? He still hadn't said anything about his plans. He would move on to whatever came next for him. She would lose him, and she'd lose Valentine, too.

Lily was holding the ladder in Dolly's hallway, while Shane installed the last light fixture. No time like the present, she thought.

"You're still coming to the shelter fund-raiser with me, right?"

He grunted, twisting the screwdriver into an uncooperative housing. "When you first asked, you didn't tell me it would be such a big deal."

"It wasn't a big deal, at first. But now, I'll be so busy, I definitely need you to handle Valentine. He performs better with you, anyway. And you want to show him off, right?"

"Do I have to dress up?"

"It's casual but don't worry, I'll look after that."

"Will there be Guinness?"

She smiled. "That can definitely be arranged."

Lily felt bad not mentioning Titan's award. She'd warned Ariel that Shane did not like surprises and that he would not appreciate being put on the spot. Ariel assured her that Shane didn't have to do anything but show up and be his own heroic self. It wasn't, she insisted, about Shane, anyway; it was about Titan, and the shelter. Shane's presence would heighten the drama of the moment, triggering maximum emotion from the audience.

It would be great for donations, Lily admitted.

Still, she felt caught between her friend and her…Shane.

At any rate, arranging the Tuxes and Tails night left her little time to think about it. But it was always there, in the back of her mind.

On the night before the event, after crossing the last item off her to-do list, she flopped onto the floor beside Valentine. He pressed up against her and thumped his tail against the hardwood.

"I'm going to miss you, buddy." Her throat closed. Shane had given no indications that he was considering adopting Valentine himself and that meant that this might be her last night with the dog. Tomorrow, if all went well, he would find his forever family. "Whoever you end up with," she said fiercely, "they better love you like…like…"

Like Shane had loved Titan.

Every dog deserved that kind of love.

Why, oh why couldn't Shane see that he and Valentine belonged together?

A decision she didn't know she'd already made crystallized in her mind.

She opened her laptop and pulled up Ariel's email address. She'd done enough favors. It was time for payback.

Hey Ariel,

You were right, okay? But not the way you think. I'm applying to adopt Valentine, but not for myself.

For Shane.

There, you weren't expecting that, were you? LOL!

A tear plopped onto the back of her hand, but she continued typing.

That dog adores him. I've watched him sit at the door waiting for Shane to come over, turning himself inside out when he hears his car in the driveway, when he hears his footstep on the path, his hand on the doorknob. How could I let him go somewhere else, knowing he'd always be pining for Shane?

Tears fell faster now. She didn't want to think about taking Valentine to the riverside park where she and Shane had first met, where he'd shared his sandwich and touched her face with his fingertip.

She pressed her palm against her jaw and closed her eyes. How would she bear it, when Shane was gone?

There will be so many people who want him once they see him on TV tomorrow and that's wonderful. But they belong together, whether Shane recognizes it or not.

If he won't accept it just yet, I'll keep Valentine with me until he does. You know I love him. But he belongs with Shane and I won't rest until he sees the truth.

Thanks, pal. I don't know what I'd do without you.

Lily

THE NEXT MORNING, the only sign of the showers that had awakened Lily in the wee hours was the mist drifting through the landscaped surroundings of the ranch. As she turned her car down the graveled driveway, she was glad that, no matter what else happened tonight, at least the Tuxes and Tails attendees wouldn't get muddy paw prints on their designer casual wear.

She drove slowly to the lot that had been roped off for the event, mindful of the box of coffee and donuts in her passenger side footwell. The volunteers had been setting up since early afternoon and the food wouldn't get there until six.

She got out and took a deep breath, finally allowing herself to believe they could pull it off. The place was perfect, the weather was perfect, everything was going according to plan and they had time to spare.

She hadn't looked forward to Valentine's Day in years but this time, she found her feelings bouncing between anticipation and dread. She'd be here with Shane. Whether it ended well or not, at least she'd be here, on a night celebrating love, with a man she cared for.

A man she loved.

She shook her head. This night wasn't about her. This was about the animals. It was about the shelter.

It was about Shane.

Shane's beloved Titan would finally get the recognition he deserved and perhaps this would allow Shane to start healing. He'd forgive her and Ariel for using his tragedy to benefit the shelter, wouldn't he?

She had to believe he would.

About keeping Valentine for him, she wasn't so sure. She

felt lighter, since making the decision. If Shane couldn't see what was right in front of him, how much he and Val needed each other, then it was up to her to show him.

But it was a risk.

Tonight would be the acting job of her life. The pretend boyfriend she'd fallen in love with hadn't fallen in love with her and now she had to pretend she was fine.

She gave her head a shake. She was fine. Or at least, she would be. She had plenty of experience with rejection. But no way was she letting him reject Valentine, too.

The sprawling rancher was built on a softly rising hillside, with a backdrop of majestic cedars and flanked by vine maples that would throw interesting shadows at sundown with their skeletal branches. Pristine white plank fences lined the driveway and several paddocks on one side. A traditional brick-red hip-roofed barn wore the name AUSTIN ACRES in big clean letters, and several smaller outbuildings were nestled nearby.

A large open riding ring lay to one side, with jumps set up on the dirt and bark mulched surface. She and Sara had taken riding lessons at a ranch like this when they were younger, until Sara turned out to be allergic.

She slid open the weathered wooden door to the building they'd co-opted for the event: the covered arena.

"Hello?"

No one heard, thanks to the deep layer of sawdust covering the floor. As her eyes adjusted from the sunshine outdoors to the dim interior light, a magical scene appeared.

Twinkle lights crisscrossed the entire ceiling. Swaths of sheer, barely there pink fabric draped gracefully in the corners. Old cotton sheets dyed a soft violet gray now provided a backdrop for small potted shrubs and hydrangeas topped with deep plum-colored blooms tied it all together.

Tall cocktail tables draped with burlap and twine held vases of the same fat hydrangeas. Straw bales were stacked for seating and photo ops and a few pieces of agility equipment were set up to show off the dogs' tricks.

At one end, the crew was putting the finishing touches on the stage. The banners had turned out beautifully, as did the informational posters set up around the arena.

It was stunning.

Romantic.

Effective, she told herself. *Keep the goals in mind.*

"There you are." Ariel came forward, wiping her hands against her cutoffs. "Well? What do you think?"

"It looks amazing." Lily walked to the stage and set the box of goodies onto a table already strewn with tools, paper, extra fabric, and whatnot. She clapped her hands. "Great work, everyone! Time for a snack."

It wouldn't be as polished as Marisa's events usually were, but this wasn't about polish. It was about having as much money as possible go directly to the shelter.

In one corner stood a huge poster board with thermometer markings and a number at the top indicating the amount required to fund the new facility. They'd be recording the donations as they came in and marking the poster accordingly with red ink throughout the evening. It was a lofty target. Would they meet it?

THREE HOURS LATER, she stood at the entrance to the arena, waiting nervously for Shane to arrive with Valentine. She'd bathed and groomed the dog before dropping him off that morning. She'd bought a new leash and harness in a coordinating plum color to match the decorations as well as her own outfit: a deep purple bias-cut tunic with three-quarter-length sleeves, black jodhpurs and black riding boots.

Guests had begun to arrive and were already milling about, sipping drinks, nibbling appetizers and looking at the photos of the adoptable pets that were pinned to the posters. Many animals would find homes tonight.

There they were.

With the setting sun behind him, she could only see Shane's outline as he walked toward her with the dog heeling calmly at his side. His posture was easy and his movements smooth. They looked like a team, perfectly matched, color coordinated and everything.

It was so obvious that they were meant to be together. All she had to do was make him see it.

"You're here," she said, forcing a smile. For tonight at least, they were hers to show off, as if the three of them were together. For reals, as Dani would say.

He stooped to kiss her cheek, bringing a light scent of

something woodsy and masculine. "You look lovely."

She swallowed. "So do you."

He'd worn the plum-colored tie she'd picked out for him, over a beautifully tailored black shirt and black jeans. He'd gotten a fresh haircut and it was styled sleekly away from his face, drawing attention to his striking bone structure.

"I know when to do as I'm told."

To cover her awkwardness, she bent down to pat Valentine. "Hello, handsome. How's my best boy?"

Valentine nuzzled against her, his tail beating against her legs. She hugged him to her and buried her face in his fresh-smelling fur. "I'm going to miss you, boy," she whispered.

But this was not the time to think about it.

She took a moment to compose her face, then stood up. She reached for the hand of the man she'd pretended to love. Somehow, she'd continue the pretense. It wasn't his fault that her love had become real. He hadn't asked for it. She hadn't intended it. She hadn't even seen it coming, had only recognized it when it was too late to back away, and all she could do was brace for heartache.

"Shall we mingle?"

Shane's eyes met hers. She couldn't read them. Did he believe her lighthearted words? Was he happy to be with her, here, right now? Or was he looking ahead to next week, eager to leave, to move on to his real life and whatever lay ahead, where there would be no reminders of the life he'd lost?

"Absolutely," he replied.

The dog barked, then jumped up, yanking at the leash.

"Val, settle," Shane said.

Instead, the dog ran around the two of them, did a spin in the air and came to a perfect sit at Shane's side.

The leash trapped them together, and Lily held Shane's arm as she freed one foot.

"What's gotten into you, Val?" He unwound the leash.

"That's Valentine, right?" A woman who'd been watching came closer. "Maybe he wants you to kiss. It's his day, after all. You know. Valentine's Day?"

She wiggled her eyebrows suggestively.

"He's a little rambunctious right now," Lily said quickly, feeling her cheeks heat. "He's smart and has excellent manners. Most rescue dogs make wonderful pets, with a little attention and training."

"Hello, Valentine." The woman reached out to pat him, and Lily waited for him to lift a paw, as he'd been taught.

Instead, he barked.

The woman jumped back, spilling her drink on her sleeve.

"Valentine!" Lily grabbed a paper napkin. "I'm so sorry. He's very friendly, just a little nervous with all the people."

"It's fine," the woman said. But her earlier warmth had grown chilly.

"Wait. Watch this. Hello, Valentine."

He looked up at Shane and whined.

"Hell-*low*, Valentine," Lily repeated, her face growing warm.

The dog stared back at her, as if he'd never heard the words before in his life.

"He really is nervous, isn't he?" the woman said, and turned away to find more promising prospects.

Lily looked at the dog. "What's the matter with you to-night?"

Valentine looked back, swept his tail against the floor, then lifted his paw perfectly.

Shane let out a laugh.

Lily glared at him. "It's not funny. He's going to be on TV. He's supposed to help us raise money for a new shelter. If he decides not to cooperate—"

She stopped and pressed the back of her hand to her mouth. She was counting on everything to go perfectly. Yes, she wanted many dogs to find loving homes because of tonight's exposure. Yes, she wanted to raise a lot of money for the shelter.

But this event was also supposed to show Marisa what her younger daughter could accomplish.

Suddenly, in her mind's eye, she saw the catastrophe it could be. A poor turnout. Out-of-control dogs tripping people, drinks spilling, guests leaving early, no one calling in with donations. No movement of the red mark on the giant thermometer on the wall.

Another red mark against the daughter who couldn't do anything right.

Lily, embarrassed yet again in front of her mother and mother's friends, and Elijah Highsmith and everyone else who'd ever laughed at her.

Shane put a hand on each shoulder and peered into her face. "Lily, whatever you're thinking, stop it."

Breath she hadn't known she was holding whooshed out of her and on the heels of it came a laugh that could just as easily have been a sob.

It was the exact advice she'd given him, and exactly what she needed to hear.

She didn't care what anyone else thought about her.

Only Shane.

"Okay," she said and took another shaky breath.

"It's going to be great, Lily. You've done a wonderful thing for the animals."

She nodded, then shook her head. "I'm freaking out, Shane," she whispered. "But not for the reasons you think."

He frowned. "What, then?"

Ariel was going to kill her. But Shane deserved at least a little warning. Especially since it wasn't the only surprise of the evening. When he found out that she'd adopted Valentine for him, she wanted him in a receptive mood.

"There's another item on the agenda." She gulped. "Promise you won't be mad."

His hands dropped from her shoulders. He took a step back. "Lily," he said in a warning tone.

"It wasn't my idea," she said, glancing around to make sure they wouldn't be overheard. "All I did was make sure that you'd be here tonight." She took a deep breath. "Shane, when Ariel found out who you were, she contacted the

Animal Heroes Society. She nominated Titan for a medal. Well, she had help from Dolly. They'll be announcing it tonight. It's a huge honor and everyone's really excited for you. It's supposed to be a surprise."

She couldn't tell a thing from his expression. It was as if he'd turned to stone, except for a small muscle ticking at the side of his mouth.

"I told Ariel that you didn't like surprises, but she said the producer insists on it. Better drama, I guess." She paused. "Are you mad?"

He looked away from her, into the growing crowd of people in the arena. "Thanks for telling me," he said, finally.

She grabbed his arm, relief coursing through her. "It was killing me, you have no idea—"

"I didn't say I wasn't mad," he said, looking at her hand.

She relinquished her hold. "I know you've got issues—"

"My issues are not the point." His eyes were flat now. "The point is, what happened that night is not for public consumption. It's not entertainment. You knew how I felt about that and you let this happen anyway. I know it's good for the shelter. It's good for the animals. Maybe you even thought it would be good for me. But that wasn't your decision to make."

He walked away then and she stood, staring after him.

This was exactly what she'd been afraid of. Maybe she should have listened to Ariel and let it happen as a surprise, so he'd just have to roll with it. Maybe that way, he'd recognize that everyone supported him, that he was the only person who thought he'd done anything wrong.

And she couldn't escape his most scathing comment, that she thought this would somehow heal him.

It was true.

She hung her head.

Hadn't her mother done the same thing to her all her life? *This is for your own good, Lily. If only you'd see that this will help you in the long run, Lily.*

People make their own choices. Shane would heal or not, in his own good time.

And he'd do it without her.

CHAPTER TWENTY

SHANE WALKED THROUGH the arena and outside into the fresh night air to the corral behind it. He leaned both hands against the wooden rail and lowered his forehead.

He couldn't believe Lily had blindsided him like this.

It wouldn't have surprised him from Gram. Even Mom.

But Lily.

Okay, so technically it was Ariel and Gram he should be mad at, not Lily. But Lily had been in on it. She could have stopped it.

He braced his hands on the rough wooden wall and dropped his head, stretching out his shoulder. He felt little pain these days, mostly stiffness.

But he still couldn't fire a gun.

He still couldn't be a cop.

Without that, he was lost.

"There you are," came a voice from the doorway.

"Gram?" He straightened up. "What are you doing here?"

"The bigger question is what are you doing here? The party's out there, sonny-boy. Or are you sulking?"

Her tone caught his attention.

"She told you, didn't she?" Gram said.

"Who told me what?" He started to move past her, but she grabbed his sleeve. She had a surprisingly sturdy grip for a woman her age.

"Lily. Your girlfriend. About the award for Titan."

He looked at her slowly. "Do you know how much I hate this?"

"Honey," she said with a laugh, "you used to hate broccoli too, but now you love it. You'll be fine."

He frowned, but she didn't let him speak.

"Yes, it'll be hard. It was an awful day and you hate reliving it. You loved that dog. You blame yourself that he's gone. Too bad. Get over it. He was a hero, just like you. Let people celebrate you both."

At the hated word, he twisted out of her grip. No one understood.

"Fine," Gram said with a huff. "Take a few minutes to pull yourself together. But know that this is happening. People out there care about you. That girl cares about you. Oh, and there's a garment bag hanging in the men's rest room for you, in case you want to do this in style."

She wagged her finger at him again for good measure and left him alone.

Shane was overreacting; he knew that. Titan deserved to be recognized for his sacrifice.

He squeezed his eyes shut tightly as memories of his dog flooded in. That big bony head, the intelligence in those dark eyes, his grace as he scaled the fence that night, his restraint in not tearing the suspect apart.

The deafening blasts. The knowledge that he'd been hit, badly. Then Titan, going after the man. Taking the bullet meant to kill him.

Titan.

He pressed his thumbs into his eye sockets as if he could push back the images but still, they came.

The way brave, powerful Titan stood head down and defeated on bath day. How he tiptoed anxiously through sliding glass doors, because he'd run into one as a puppy and had never gotten over it. How he'd kept a ragged stuffed bunny in his crate for comfort.

He waited for the rush of pain that always accompanied the memories. But it didn't come.

He lifted his head. "Huh," he said into the night air.

Somewhere to his left, a horse snorted, and a shadow moved.

More images arrived: Titan, leaping into the air to catch a Frisbee. Digging in the garden. Play-bowing an invitation to a game of tag with his doggy friends. Doing all the normal, ordinary things that dogs did, when given the opportunity.

He thought about the training center in Alberta, where he and Titan had met. He'd told himself that he'd never be able to love another dog like Titan.

But Valentine had surprised him. This animal of indeterminable ancestry, who'd known nothing but neglect, who'd been repeatedly abandoned, who'd been introduced to training at well past the optimal age, had turned out to be an overflowing well of ability.

That, he realized now, was the real challenge. The long odds.

Titan had been perfect. He'd done his job like a soldier, and his ability to communicate, to anticipate situations and respond appropriately, had been uncanny. They'd been a unit, trained together, served together.

Fallen together.

Only when Titan went down that last time, he stayed down.

"Easy, Valentine," came a voice behind him.

He turned to see Lily, with the dog straining toward him at the end of the leash.

"Sorry to interrupt, but he's going crazy without you." Lily stopped a few feet away from him. "I know I'm not exactly your favorite person right now, but please don't shut Valentine out. He doesn't understand."

In the dim light, he could see the sparkle of unshed tears in her eyes.

He hunkered down and opened his arms. The dog nearly bowled him over, climbing on him, licking him, ecstatic at finding him once more.

He was going to miss this big mutt, he realized. Whoever adopted Valentine better be prepared to be the best damn dog owner on the planet, because this dog deserved nothing less.

Lily and Ariel would make sure of that, but would they

follow up? Would they visit him in a year to be certain it was working out? He couldn't bear the thought of Valentine's heart being broken yet again, of his spirit languishing alone and neglected in a backyard somewhere.

"We should join the others," Lily said softly. "If you're staying, that is. They'll be announcing the award in about a half hour. It'll be an awkward moment for Ariel if you're not here to accept it."

"I'm staying," he said.

This was Valentine's shot at getting the very best home, and Shane would keep his word and do his part to make it happen.

And when the time came for Titan's award, he'd handle it with grace.

"I'm sorry I was a jerk," he said suddenly. "You were right. I have issues. I hate the word hero. You know why Titan died? Because he disobeyed me. If I'd been a better trainer, a better leader, he'd have stopped when I ordered him to. But I let up on him. I wasn't as firm as I should have been. That's why I didn't want to train Valentine. That's why I don't have another dog. That's why I can't talk about Titan."

He'd never said those words aloud. He'd barely allowed himself to think them. They'd been inside him, getting larger every day, crushing him, suffocating him.

Suddenly, he could breathe.

Lily stepped closer, placed her hand tentatively on his arm. "Shane." Her voice broke. "I'm sorry too. We had no right to leverage your experience for this event, on how much attention it may attract."

That's all it was now. An experience. It didn't define him. It didn't have to hold him back any longer.

"Split the difference?" He touched her cheek, knuckled away a tear. "At least you warned me."

She gave a choking laugh. "They might have gotten more drama than they wanted."

He cupped her chin. "So you got it, instead."

"I can take it." She put her soft warm palm over his. "I'm tough."

She was tough. Tough enough to love him, even when he gave her no hope of having it returned, even when he'd never spoken of the future. Tough enough to take in a dog like Valentine, throw her whole heart into him and then say goodbye.

He bent down to touch her lips, but she moved her hand to block him.

"No," she whispered. "Please don't."

He closed his eyes and pressed his forehead against hers. "I'm sorry. I don't know what I was thinking. Are we still pretending? Or pretending to pretend?"

"I think," Lily said, "that it's time to just be ourselves, for a change."

The quiver in her voice made his chest hurt. She didn't know what she was asking.

"I'M A BAD bet, Lily." The Adam's apple in Shane's throat jumped. "It's not just the bum arm or the fact that I don't know what I'll be doing next month, let alone next year."

She had a bad feeling about what he was going to say.

"I was engaged to a woman I'd known for ten years." He swallowed again. "Childhood sweethearts. Maybe I always knew something was wrong and that's why I wouldn't set a date. I don't know. But after the…incident…" He shook his head. "I didn't feel anything. She was so grateful that I was alive and all I could think was that I'd lost my best friend. I realized that she didn't understand about Titan. She didn't understand my work. She didn't understand me." He sucked in a deep shuddering breath. "It took a brush with death for me to wake up and see that I was marrying my high-school girlfriend not because she was the love of my life but because everyone expected it. It would have been a huge mistake and I didn't see it."

He looked at her with hot, tortured intensity and something more.

Regret.

He cared for her. Maybe he even loved her. Or could, if he'd let himself.

Her breath quickened. His words unlocked something inside her. An old memory, a snippet of conversation she hadn't understood at the time, came back to her.

Her parents. In the hospital.

She closed her eyes. She didn't like to think of that time. The pain of losing her father had been unbearable. She'd been so angry.

"What is it?" he asked.

"I've never had much luck with romance either," she said, taking his hand. "But instead of one failed long-term relationship, I've had lots of failed short-term ones. My dad died when I was twelve and I've always figured that somehow it left me with a deep, dark inability to trust." She gave a little laugh. "So, you could say we're both bad bets."

"He couldn't help dying," Shane said.

Lily frowned. "I know." There was a buzzing in her ears, like flies trapped inside a bottle.

"What happened to him?" Shane's expression had changed to one of concern. He wasn't asking from ghoulish curiosity. He understood from experience that talking about it, as awful as it was, helped. "Lily?"

She shrugged away his arm. "I'm okay. We don't talk about this stuff much." She exhaled. "He had a heart attack."

"Oh," Shane said. "I'm sorry."

She shook her head again. "That was his brush with death, you could say."

He looked at her quizzically.

"He was killed later in a construction accident," she said, repeating the words they'd all spoken so many times. It was the truth. He'd fallen from hastily erected scaffolding. The evidence had been clear.

"The part my mother doesn't talk about," she said, feeling terrified and exhilarated all at once, "is that once he'd recovered from the heart attack, he left us. Just like your wake-up call. Only he had a wife and family."

There. She'd said it.

Her dad had left them.

Left her.

INSIDE THE ARENA, people were having a wonderful time. Lily's face transformed and no one but him would have known that she was smiling around a bruised heart.

The dogs they'd chosen to bring to the event were freshly groomed and on their best behavior. The little Shih Tzu cross with the missing eye had everyone laughing when he sat up and begged for a treat. The red-nosed pit bull with the pink bow on her collar ran through the agility course like a champ and then sang her woo-woo song at the end. The shaggy black collie-Lab retrieved a series of dumbbells to great applause.

Only Valentine refused to cooperate. Oh, he walked beautifully on the leash. He sat. He stayed. He lay down on command. But whenever Shane introduced him to someone and gave the "shake a paw" command, the dog looked at him like he was speaking a foreign language.

Finally, he took him outside for a break. "What's the matter with you, boy? This is your chance to really impress people. There might be a family out there just waiting for a dog like you and you act as if you don't even care. You're not shy. You love people. I don't understand."

Valentine sat and held out a paw.

Shane palmed his forehead. "Yup. Perfect. I don't get it."

The dog watched him with dark, pleading eyes.

And just like that, Shane understood.

Valentine wasn't on his best behavior tonight because he wasn't trying to impress anyone.

He'd already found his forever home.

Oh, no.

"Come on, boy," he said. He had to find Ariel. He had to let her know that this dog wasn't going anywhere.

CHAPTER TWENTY-ONE

LILY LOOKED ACROSS to where Marisa's harpist, who'd left her harp at home, was playing pop country tunes on her acoustic guitar.

Instead of the black evening gown that was her customary costume at Kovac Foundation events, she wore gray leather pants, a white, western-styled shirt, bright red boots and a black cowboy hat.

Everyone had layers, hidden surprises, if you knew where to look.

When she'd caught the musician's attention, Lily drew her finger across her throat and pointed to the makeshift stage.

Here goes, she thought.

"Attention everyone," Ariel said, clapping her hands. She'd polished up for the occasion, wearing a long, fitted denim skirt and chunky-heeled boots.

She gripped the mic with two hands and surveyed the crowd. "What do you get when you put hundreds of the lower mainland's most passionate animal lovers together in one place, here at beautiful Austin Acres on the most romantic night of the year?"

A cheer went up from the crowd.

"That's right! You get a lot of heart. A lot of pet hair, too. But we're used to that, aren't we?"

Laughter rippled over the arena.

"As many of you know," she went on, her expression growing serious, "our existing building flooded earlier this year, causing a difficult disruption in care. With the help of an army of dedicated volunteers, we cleaned up as best we could. The animals were all relocated to foster homes or shelters in nearby municipalities, but after assessing the damage, the board decided that the aging building must be replaced. Tonight is about meeting that need." She faced the camera and smiled. "Channel twelve is filming tonight and has generously offered to match every dollar designated for the new facility."

The arena exploded with a roar of approval.

Mother's events were never this noisy. Lily wondered what the more staid contingent thought of this benefit they'd been dragged or guilted into attending.

"I'm also delighted to announce," Ariel went on, "that Marisa Rollins from the Kovac Foundation has pledged ongoing support for our efforts. A huge thank you to Ms. Rollins and her many friends who've joined us tonight. With all of us working together, Maple Grove Animal Shelter will continue to help animals in need in our community."

She stepped off the podium to another round of applause.

Lily felt faint. Marisa was supporting the shelter?

Ariel rushed up to Lily, her hair bouncing. "Donations are pouring in. Have you seen the interaction with our animal ambassadors? Everyone wants to take them home. This is our most successful fund-raiser, ever."

"My mom pledged support?" Lily asked. "When did that happen?"

Ariel shrugged. "When I asked. Her friends are cool, too. Not as uptight as I thought they'd be. I think that guy in the polka dots has his name in for Suzy-One-Eye."

She followed Ariel's finger. "Elijah Highsmith wants to adopt a half-blind Shih Tzu!?"

"You know what they say. The heart wants what the heart wants," Ariel said. "Oh! Time for Titan's award!"

She bounced away, leaving Lily in confusion. She'd spoken with a few people who'd previously seemed cold and intimidating to her. Tonight, they seemed different, friendlier, even expressing appreciation for her efforts.

Had she misjudged her mother's friends?

Had she misjudged her mother?

A tall, elegantly dressed woman approached the dais and tapped the microphone.

"Hello, everyone," she said. "My name is Eloise Frampton and I'm the president of the Animal Heroes Society. I know that all of our beloved pets are heroes in their own way, even if all they do is act goofy to make us smile after a hard day."

Laughter rippled over the crowd.

"But sometimes, truly remarkable things happen. Each

year we recognize companion animals that have gone above and beyond in service to their humans and tonight, we have a very special award."

The arena dimmed to just the twinkle lights. A screen appeared with an image of Titan on it, with his full name, and the performance titles he'd earned. One by one, more images appeared. Titan leaping over a wall. Titan in his bulletproof vest. Titan chasing a ball. Titan looking up at Shane, his pink tongue lolling out, a goofy doggy grin on his face, adoration in every line of his body.

Lily swallowed. She knew just how he felt.

"Police Service Dog Titan," Eloise Frampton continued, "worked with a human partner who earlier this year was also recognized for his dedication and bravery. Sergeant Bowman, will you join me please?"

Lily held her breath as she looked around. When Shane took the rough stage, a low ahhh of approval sounded from the audience.

Instead of the black-and-plum outfit he'd been wearing earlier, he now appeared in full dress uniform, the red serge jacket, the hat, the boots, everything. Dolly, she thought, shaking her head.

At his side was Valentine, alert but obedient.

Her heart swelled with pride, for both of them. She pressed her clasped hands against her mouth. Shane looked spectacular, breathtaking. In her mind, he'd been a hero from the moment they'd met. Even in his dusty flannel shirt and ripped jeans, he couldn't be anything but a hero.

Shane took his place under the spotlight and motioned for Valentine to sit. Then he looked up, scanning the audience.

When his eyes landed on her, his face relaxed. He smiled. Took a breath.

Lily smiled back. He wasn't hers, but that was okay. He was a gift to the world. She'd get over him. Somehow.

Maybe.

Eloise Frampton gave a brief history of Shane's relationship with the dog, their training and work together. She described the night of the shooting, in crisp, factual language, nothing florid or sentimental, nothing designed to manipulate the emotions of her listeners. Only deep respect.

Then she turned to Shane.

"Sergeant Bowman," she said. "On behalf of the Animal Heroes Society and the citizens of British Columbia, please accept our gratitude to you and PSD Titan for your service. Titan was a true animal hero and his sacrifice will be remembered."

She handed him a simple statue and shook his hand. Applause filled the room. Flashbulbs sparkled as people with cell phones captured the moment for their social media feeds.

"For Titan!" someone yelled.

"For Titan!"

Shane stepped up to the mic and motioned for quiet.

"Thank you. I'm touched and honored more than I can say." He cleared his throat, swallowed, the effort this speech was costing him evident. "I haven't spoken much about Titan since he passed. There are a lot of reasons, but mostly, it just hurt too damn much." He looked down at Valentine, took a breath. "This animal sitting next to me is no police dog. He doesn't have a spotless pedigree or a background of careful, deliberate training. In fact, he arrived at the shelter damaged in every way, ignored, neglected, forgotten, discarded. He couldn't be more unlike Titan. His name, Valentine, is something no self-respecting police officer would ever call his partner."

Valentine barked. Shane smiled and waited for the chuckles in the crowd to fade.

"But like Titan, this dog is also a hero." Shane looked across the room and found Lily once more. "Working with him reminded me that while losing Titan was a senseless tragedy, it didn't take away from all the good times we had, or all the great things Titan accomplished in his short life. When we met, Valentine and I were both lost and broken. Without the persistence of a very special woman, we might have stayed there. But now, thanks to her, Valentine is ready to move on to the next stage of his life, a permanent home, with someone who will love him the way he deserves to be loved. We should all be so lucky. Lily Garner, you are a heroine to us both."

Cheers rose from every corner. The spotlight twirled around until it landed on her face, blinding her. Pats and hugs and congratulations came at her from all sides.

When she could focus again, she saw, two tables away,

her mother, clapping fiercely, tears in her eyes. Marisa's platinum-blonde hair was shiny and straight. Despite an understated ensemble of tailored slacks and twin set, she was every inch her usual regal self.

Except for the glow of pride on her face.

And the pledge of support for the shelter.

It was a night full of surprises.

CHAPTER TWENTY-TWO

WHEN THE AWARDS were over and denim-vested waitstaff began circulating with cupcakes and brownies, Lily pulled herself away from the damp hugs. Shane was still trapped by a never-ending cluster of well-wishers, his red coat flickering like a beacon as people came and went.

She saw Marisa standing beside the exercise pen where Valentine was taking a well-earned nap, a plastic flute of sparkling water in her hand. The photographer approached. She gave him a practiced smile, then saw Lily and waved her over.

A mother-daughter photo op.

Lily checked the skin beneath her eyes for signs of moisture, then stepped between partygoers to meet her mom, arranging her expression.

The little girl inside her was a two-faced child, her lifelong companion of sun and shadow, one moment a smiling optimist, reaching for the trophy of parental approval and at the next, a sadist, hurling toward unbreachable obstacles, unable to quit the race.

"Not quite your usual scene, is it?" Lily stood next to her

mother, close enough that their upper arms brushed. Music played again and around them, conversation and laughter buzzed, the sound dropping softly into the sawdust beneath them, creating an atmosphere of intimacy.

"Definitely not," Marisa agreed. "But that's not to say I haven't enjoyed myself."

"I'm glad to hear it."

Elijah Highsmith spied them and quickly came over, his own camera hanging from a strap around his neck.

Lily braced herself.

"Marisa, darling," he said. "What a delightful change of pace."

They exchanged cheek kisses. Elijah ignored Lily completely.

"I'm glad you're enjoying yourself," Marisa said, her tone unreadable. "Would you like a mother-daughter photo?"

Elijah drew back from the lens. "Sara's here?"

Lily waved into his face. "Hi, Elijah."

He blinked. "Of course, Millie, yes. Smile, ladies."

Lily crossed her arms. He may have redeemed himself slightly with Suzy-One-Eye, but Lily'd had enough of his slights. At some point, you had to stick up for yourself, whatever the cost.

"It's Lily. Not Millie. Shall I spell it?" *You pretentious asshat.* She only added the words mentally, but something in her tone must have given them away.

The words she *had* spoken left her mouth during a conversational lull, landing like a bold, above-the-fold, all-caps headline. Silence followed. It probably only lasted a second or two, but it felt like an eternity.

Then Elijah's mouth parted, wordlessly. He whirled to face Marisa, prepared to launch a complaint.

Here we go, thought Lily.

But Marisa cut him off. "You're a dear friend, Elijah. But sometimes you can be..." She gave an eloquent shrug that underscored Lily's own sentiment beautifully.

Elijah gaped like a stranded fish and Lily had to bite the inside of her cheek to keep from laughing. A titter sounded from behind them.

Marisa rose to her full height. "My daughter, Lily Garner. The heroine Shane mentioned in his speech. The woman who organized this event, and saved Valentine's life. You've met her before. Several times."

Now it was Lily's turn to gape. Her mother, defending her?

"I remember now." Elijah swallowed hard and dipped his head. "I'm sorry for my behavior, Lily. There's no excuse for my ignorance. Will you allow me to take your photograph? You should be very proud of what you've achieved tonight."

"Thank you, Elijah." He looked truly remorseful and she decided to give him another chance. "Are you really adopting Suzy?"

Excitement bloomed on his face. "I am. I had a dog just like her when I was a boy." He glanced at Marisa. "I never thought of adopting a shelter animal, but the moment I saw her, I knew I had to bring her home. Thank you. Lily."

She held out her hand and after a momentary hesitation, he took it and they shook.

"Now," Lily said, "make us look like a million bucks."

"Wait!" Marisa lifted the latch on Valentine's pen, then dropped gracefully beside him. "Come on, honey. Valentine needs some love."

Lily bent down, put one arm over the ecstatic dog and leaned her head in. "You never fail to amaze me, Mother."

They smiled and mugged and accepted sloppy doggy kisses while Elijah captured the moment and then moved on to other subjects.

Marisa patted Valentine, then straightened up and brushed a minute spot of dust off her pant leg. "You've surprised me tonight, too, Lily."

"Telling Elijah where to get off? I should have done it months ago."

"Probably." Marisa smoothed her hair. "But I meant this whole evening. I confess I didn't expect such an enthusiastic response. You've hit on something people really care about. And everyone is having a wonderful time."

"Oh. Well. We had so much help." She struggled to find the right words. "I don't know how to thank you. You went above and beyond with your support, Mom. I had no idea you intended to become a donor. It's…amazing."

"As are you, my dear." Marisa adjusted her earrings, then turned to face Lily, her expression serious. "As is your Shane. He's quite something, a hero, as they say."

The sound of his name brought a swift sharp stab to her

heart. "He is. But he's not mine. He never really was."

"Are you sure about that?"

Lily blew breath through pursed lips. "I'm not sure of anything. I don't think he is, either."

"It's Valentine's Day, dear. Maybe you should let yourself go with it."

"That doesn't sound like you." Lily smiled.

Marisa put a hand to her neck. "People can change."

Shane cared for her, Lily believed. But he had so much to figure out about his life. He would discover his own path, in his own time. If it led back to her, one day—

No. She had to let him go.

She pulled her shoulders up high. "I should go. There's a great deal of cleanup and if I don't want to be here all night, I should get started."

"Wait." Marisa touched manicured fingers to Lily's arm. She looked, again, near tears. "Darling, did you mean what you said that day, about how working with me made you miserable?"

Never once had Lily imagined that her words would have had an effect of this kind on her mother, that they would have penetrated any more than water off a duck.

"Mom." Lily stroked her arm, then pulled her into a hug. "I didn't mean to hurt you."

"Then it's true."

She pulled away and looked into her mother's eyes, seeing, maybe for the first time, the cracks in the facade. "You seem to need someone with different skills," she said carefully. "And I don't like disappointing you."

Marisa blinked rapidly, the tendons in her throat working. "You always were your father's daughter."

"And Sara was yours."

"Did it ever occur to you," Marisa said, "that maybe I was trying to find a way in? That having you with me at the Kovac Foundation was a way to spend time with you?"

Lily frowned. "You needed someone to fill in for Sara."

Marisa shook her head impatiently. "Anyone could do what she does. I wanted to have my daughter, my other daughter, at my side."

Lily had no idea how to respond.

Marisa, now on a roll, went on. "Don't you think I knew how hurt you were when your father left us? More than Sara. More even than me, I think. Did it ever occur to you that I wanted to fill that gap, to help heal that wound?"

Marisa looked up and waved gaily to someone across the room, as if they weren't having a heart-to-heart conversation in the middle of an animal shelter fund-raiser, then continued, her voice low and shaking. "I may appear to be shallow and self-centered, but when a mother hears her child cry every night for months, she can't help but feel responsible. I wanted to comfort you. I tried. I've always tried. But you only wanted him. And in your mind, I drove him away. So. Here we are."

Lily felt as if her knees might crumple along with the lies her childhood had been built upon.

"I'm proud of you, you know," Marisa continued. "Perhaps I don't say it enough. Perhaps I've never said it. But I am. You are so much…more…than I've ever been." She shook her head, wonderingly. "You've got drive, determination. You've got passion and a will to get what you want out of life and you don't care what people think. I've always envied you that."

If Lily got to be a hundred years old, she'd never be more surprised by anything in her life. Her mother, envious of her?

"Oh, Mom," Lily said. She tugged the older woman into her embrace. Marisa's bones were too near the surface, her body frailer than Lily realized. "Just when I think I've got you pegged you go and say something like that."

This time the sniff was more of a snort, a sound so atypical of Marisa Rollins that Lily had to laugh.

"You've been bored by me since you were two years old," Marisa said. "I couldn't keep you clean for five seconds together. All you wanted was to be outside in the dirt or up to your elbows in paint or clay or sawdust."

She was crying now. Which made Lily cry. "I always thought you'd divided us up, the pretty daughter for you, the awkward tomboy for Dad."

"Honey." Marisa stroked Lily's hair, looking at her with moist, sparkling eyes. "You weren't an awkward tomboy. I think somehow, you sensed that your father wasn't happy. You always were intuitive, much more so than Sara. But it was never your responsibility to fix us. Your father and I…it would have ended sooner or later, I suppose. But I'm so sorry it happened the way it did. It was a horrible time. I believe that of the three of us, his death hurt you the most."

Lily couldn't speak. They'd never discussed her father. It was a forbidden topic. But Marisa, once started, seemed determined to continue.

"And now you're giving me orders, putting me in my place and starting your own business. Your father would be proud, you know. And one last thing. Don't be so sure about Shane." Marisa paused, then stroked her daughter's cheek. "You've got stakes all over that rough territory. He just might not know it yet."

"WHAT DO YOU mean, he's already spoken for?" Shane followed Ariel to the leader board, where she had to rise onto her tiptoes to mark the next level of donations with her red pen.

"I'm sorry, Shane, but an ideal applicant has already been accepted. We've got adoption counselors talking with people over there."

She pointed to a couple of tables, where shelter volunteers were indeed sitting with several people with eager expressions on their faces.

"But, Ariel," he said, "I want to adopt him for Lily. It's Lily! And me! Valentine knows us. Find your applicant a different dog."

"There may be," she said, "a way to work things out. With the adoptive owner. This is highly unusual, but he's been one of the most difficult placements I've ever handled. Come with me."

He followed her through the crowd, out of the arena to a small room at the back of the stables. Riding equipment lined the walls and it smelled of leather and horses.

To his surprise, Lily was standing in the corner, clutching her elbows.

"What are you doing here?" he said.

"I'm trying to do what's best for Valentine," she said, tears in her voice. "But I've messed it all up. I wanted to adopt him, Shane. Not for myself. I wanted to give him to you."

His mouth dropped open. He looked at Ariel. She motioned impatiently at Lily.

"I know, you said you didn't want him," Lily continued, "but he loves you so much, I thought if I did this, you wouldn't be able to say no. You wouldn't want to break his heart. I know you've got a lot of decisions ahead of you, and maybe it's the wrong time to have a dog in your life, but I knew that if he was with you, he'd always be safe and happy." Her voice cracked. "But now he's going to someone else and everything's ruined!"

She dissolved in tears, putting her head in her hands.

Ariel quietly cleared her throat.

Shane looked between her and Lily, finally understanding. "You?"

Ariel exhaled. "Someone had to do something. It's been painful, watching the two of you. For heaven's sake, put her out of her misery."

She squeezed his arm, then left the room, closing the door softly behind her.

Shane pulled up a wooden stool next to the weeping woman who was so full of love he didn't know how he hadn't recognized it before.

"Lily, honey," he said, taking her hand in his. "I applied to adopt him, too. For you."

She lifted her head. "What?"

He laughed softly. "I guess we both had the same idea. We can't let that mutt go to yet another home. He's already home. He has been since the day you brought him there in your car."

She pressed her fingers against her forehead. "But...he loves you."

"Lily," he said. "You underestimate...yourself."

He hesitated, uncertain of the boundaries of their relationship. She was so independent, so determined not to need anyone, especially a man.

Especially him.

And he'd gone along with it. He didn't want to have his heart torn out again and the only way to stay truly safe was to stay completely apart.

Only it hadn't gone that way with Lily. And now here they were. Not apart.

But not together, either.

So where did that leave him?

"All night," she said presently, "people have been surprising me. Things I thought and believed turned out to be not quite right. It's as if the lines I've been coloring in my whole life suddenly turned out to be in the wrong book." Melancholy wove through her voice.

"Lily?"

"You know. When you realize that the narrative running through your story, the—" she frowned, impatient for him to understand "—the framework, the thing you hold on to when you don't know what you're doing, is actually full of holes."

He tipped his head sideways. "I might. Go on."

She turned and faced him in the dim light. "Here I was, going through my life thinking I was one thing, my sister was another, my mother, someone else yet and my father…well. Point is, I was wrong."

She shook her head slowly, wonderingly. She met his gaze. "I was wrong about so much."

"Oh, honey." Shane laced his fingers through hers, feeling the pulse at her wrist, tripping way too fast.

Glints of gold and red danced in her hair, starlight catching the brightness of random strands. She looked like an angel, haloed and precious, valiant and powerful and wise.

He thought of the kiss they'd shared the night of the awards gala and knew suddenly that he'd been the worst kind of fool. When he was at his lowest, she'd taken him in her arms, pressed her lips on his and brought light and warmth to the cold dark places in his heart. And what had he done?

He'd let her go.

"You weren't wrong about me. You saw through me," he said. "You made me face the truth."

"And what is that?" She was so close that he could feel the warmth of her breath. "What truth did I make you see, Shane?"

She moved her hand out from under his and laid it against his heart. It sat like a brand, searing him, marking him, burning away the pretense, all the way down to blood and bone.

Truth.

Sudden terror filled him. Far worse than feeling Titan's hot blood on his hands, worse than the dawning knowledge of broken dreams, this was a terror of possibility. Of potential.

"You made me see myself differently, Shane," Lily continued. "That changed everything. I stood up to my mom. I stood up to Elijah. I don't even know when or how I decided, it just happened. Because I'm not the same woman I was when we met. I chased love for so long, not even knowing what it looked like. Then, when I found it, it seemed too good to be true. It was too good to be true. Neither one of us wanted to believe that something so good could also be true."

Hope vied with terror and stuck in his throat. He couldn't breathe, let alone speak.

"Valentine brought us together, Shane. But this..." She pressed against his chest. "This heart of yours has captured me. Whatever happens next, remember that. You are a gift.

Our time together has been a miracle. I don't expect anything of you." She swallowed. "Well, I expect you're going to move on to whatever comes next for you. I wish our hearts were at the same place at the same time, but I can't help it that you're so far behind me."

A laugh that could have been a sob triggered an answering sound from him. Sometimes words weren't necessary.

With a rough cry, he bent his head and captured her mouth. Instantly, she was in his arms, as if she'd always belonged there, and always would, from before the stars were in the sky and long after the earth's last dying groans.

CHAPTER TWENTY-THREE

WHEN HE'D ARRIVED in Maple Grove all those months ago, Shane never thought he'd end up staying.

He never dreamed he'd end up with a rescue dog at his side.

He certainly never dreamed that that rescue dog would come with a woman attached, a woman who, it turned out, had captured his heart long before he'd recognized the fact.

He and Lily sat at the bench overlooking the river, near Gram's house, where they'd first met.

Valentine lay quietly at Lily's feet. He seemed to know that he no longer had to choose between the two of them.

Gram had shocked him to his socks when, instead of posting a For Sale sign in her front yard, she'd handed him the deed to the house.

He'd shocked himself by accepting it. There were strings, of course. He had to turn the front room into a home office for his new business. And he had to name that business Titan Dog Training. And he had to sublet the rest the house to an as-yet unnamed design firm made up of Lily, Harpreet and Danika.

"You know," Lily said. "I used to hate Valentine's Day."

"Did you?"

"I think it started in first grade, when Jimmy Belyk gave everyone but me a card." She laughed. "Things only went downhill from there. Then I swore off dating, and I finally had a Valentine's Day worth remembering."

"And what about dating?" he asked.

"I'm still done with that." She leaned her head against his shoulder. "I mean, unless you need a pretend girlfriend again at some point."

"Nope. I'm swearing off pretend girlfriends. Only the real thing for me." Shane looked at her. "What are we doing, then? If we're not calling it dating?"

She looked at him. "You tell me."

He leaned over and kissed her gently. "Definitely not dating."

"Absolutely not."

He sat back and then reached into the pocket of his blue jeans. "I have something for you."

Her eyes lit up. "Really?"

"It's nothing much," he said, as he pulled out a small velvet box. "But I think you'll like it."

"What's the occasion?" she asked, taking the box.

"Open it."

Inside she found a necklace. A thin gold chain with three pendants on it. One a locket in the shape of a heart, one embossed with the impression of a shaggy dog that looked remarkably like Valentine, and one a delicately wrought floating heart.

"Happy Valentine's Day," he said. "Sorry it's a little late." He opened the locket. On one side, he had a photo of himself with the dog. On the other, a photo of Lily.

"Oh, Shane!" She laughed and held it up for a closer look. "It's beautiful. I love it. I love *you*."

"You're beautiful and I love you." He put the chain around her neck and closed the clasp. "From now on, until the end of time, Valentine's Day will be the best day of the year. You may have had some rough ones. Just like our boy. But we had to go through those, to get to this."

He bent down and patted the dog. He was the luckiest man in the world.

"The best part of my life began on that day," Lily said. "Because I found a dog called Valentine."

The End

If you enjoyed *A Dog Called Valentine*, you'll love these other Roxanne Snopek romances…

The Montana Home series

Book 1: Her Montana Hero

Book 2: A Sweet Montana Christmas

Book 3: The Cowboy Next Door

Book 4: Cinderella's Cowboy

Available now at your favorite online retailer!

About the Author

USA TODAY bestselling author Roxanne Snopek writes contemporary romance both sexy and sweet, in small towns, big cities and secluded islands, with families and communities that will warm your heart. Her fictional heroes (like her own real-life hero) are swoon-worthy, uber-responsible, secretly vulnerable and occasionally dough-headed, but animals love them, which makes everything okay. Roxanne writes from British Columbia, Canada, where she is surrounded by wild flowers, wildlife and animals that require regular feeding. She does yoga to stay sane. It works, mostly.

Thank you for reading

A Dog Called Valentine

If you enjoyed this book, you can find more from all our great authors at TulePublishing.com, or from your favorite online retailer.

Made in the USA
Middletown, DE
12 February 2019

No good deed goes unpunished.

When an unwanted Valentine's Day present is dumped at the shelter, volunteer Lily decides to foster the poor dog herself. A little attention is all he needs to blossom into a loving pet, ready for his forever home. Plus, helping a poor, rejected animal will distract her from her own problems. Win, win. Right? Wrong. Valentine needs more than a makeover if he's going to be adopted. He destroys her home, hates to be groomed and when he behaves better for a perfect stranger than he does her, Lily swallows her pride and begs the good looking but quiet stranger for help.

After losing his canine partner in a horrific moment that upended his future, sexy and stoic Shane turns to books, walks in the park and remodeling his grandmother's home. No more intense K9 officer career, no more dogs, no more risks. But it's hard to ignore the misunderstood mutt at the park and his well-intentioned, but clueless, handler. Shane reluctantly agrees to give her a few tips and tricks, but that's all. He won't care. He won't get invested. And once Valentine finds his new home, his life can go back to normal.

But Shane doesn't bargain on a new normal in town and, suddenly, Valentine's Day will never be the same.

Born under a Scorpio moon, raised in a little house on the prairie, USA Today Bestselling Author Roxanne Snopek said "as you wish" to her Alpha Farm Boy and followed him to the mountain air and ocean breezes of British Columbia. There, while healing creatures great and small and raising three warrior-princesses, they found their real-life happily-ever-after. After also establishing a successful freelance and non-fiction career, Roxanne began writing what she most loved to read: romance.